THE BOOK OF PEARL

TIMOTHÉE DE FOMBELLE

WALKER
BOOKS

This is a work of fiction. Names, characters, places and incidents
are either the product of the author's imagination or, if real, used
fictitiously. All statements, activities, stunts, descriptions, information
and material of any other kind contained herein are included for
entertainment purposes only and should not be relied on for
accuracy or replicated as they may result in injury.

First published in Great Britain 2016 by Walker Books Ltd
87 Vauxhall Walk, London SE11 5HJ

2 4 6 8 10 9 7 5 3 1

Text © 2014 Gallimard Jeunesse
English Translation © 2016 Sarah Ardizzone and Sam Gordon
Cover illustration © 2016 Mike Bennion

The right of Timothée de Fombelle and Sarah Ardizzone, Sam Gordon
to be identified as author and translators respectively of this
work has been asserted by them in accordance with the
Copyright, Designs and Patents Act 1988

This book has been typeset in Sabon

Printed and bound in Denmark by Nørhaven

British Library Cataloguing in Publication Data:
a catalogue record for this book is available from the British Library

ISBN 978-1-4063-6462-0

www.walker.co.uk

THE
BOOK
OF
PEARL

BY
TIMOTHÉE DE FOMBELLE

Translated by
Sarah Ardizzone and Sam Gordon

INSTITUT
FRANÇAIS
ROYAUME-UNI

This boo͏k ... i as part
o ... .

ALSO BY TIMOTHÉE DE FOMBELLE:

Toby Alone
Toby and the Secrets of the Tree
Vango: Between Sky and Earth
Vango: A Prince Without a Kingdom

Every time a child says, 'I don't believe in fairies,'
there is a fairy somewhere that falls down dead.
– J.M. Barrie, *Peter Pan*

Contents

Part One
A Passenger in the Storm

1   Far From the Kingdoms   13
2   Between my Tears   23
3   The Refuge   32
4   The Girl   41
5   Treasure   48
6   Small Ghosts   58
7   The Castaway   70
8   The Opening   82
9   Once Upon a Time   95
10   The Source of the Lake   104
11   Metamorphosis   115
12   Love   126

Part Two
Keeping Grief Alive

13   Joshua Iliån Pearl   135
14   The Mermaid's Scale   145
15   Like a Little Snake   155
16   The Train   167

17 A Fleeting Glimpse   176

18 Flight   187

19 Under the Almond Trees   196

20 The Blue Slipper   206

21 Until the Fighting is Over   216

22 Sorceress   225

23 In the Chamber   237

Part Three

Lost Fragments from the Kingdoms

24 Bastille Day Ball   253

25 Memories   265

26 Old Before his Time   277

27 The Collection   288

28 Blood and Ruin   300

29 The Life of Oliå   311

30 The First Book of Pearl   325

31 An Apparition   337

32 The Eternal Palace   349

33 The Last Archer   359

Part One

A PASSENGER IN THE STORM

1

FAR FROM THE KINGDOMS

Who could have guessed that she used to be a fairy? She had escaped from the tower window by ripping up her clothes to make a rope. Is that how fairies are supposed to descend from the ramparts? She was wearing the long white shift that she had stolen afterwards, from a washing line stretched out under the moon. She was running across the sand and through the night. The day before, she had renounced all her powers. Now she looked just like any other girl her age, only ever so slightly more lost, more sensitive, more beautiful.

The beach was white and wide. Above it, the dark of the forests; and below, the rolling waves, the spray of the surf and everywhere, the sound of the sea, the warmth of a night more luminous than day.

Her feet didn't sink in as she ran over the wet sand,

but each step made a ring of water around her that teemed with tiny crabs. She was on the brink of collapse and had no idea what time it was: she just knew that at midnight it would all be over.

He would be dead.

The day before, she could have glided effortlessly over the foam, or flown above the forests, to reach him more swiftly.

The day before, she had been a fairy.

But for that same reason, the day before, she couldn't have shared in the destiny of the person she loved; she couldn't have lived or died with him. Which was why she had renounced her magical powers, although, even in the oldest tales it was almost unheard of for a fairy to abdicate in this way.

Far off, the gleam from the lightship shone less brightly, glowing red at the end of a black stone jetty that linked it to the land. Whole trees were burned in this copper-lined vessel in order to attract boats from other realms, only to dash them against the rocks. That was where he had been taken to endure his fate.

The distance separating the stretch of sand from the red eye of the lightship seemed infinitely far.

She was running by the water's edge now, gasping,

caught in a tunnel between the slope of the beach and the warm wind blowing in off the sea. She was learning about the trials of the flesh, about injured feet, breathlessness, and the frailty of the body: the human condition she had so craved. She was in pain, but had no regrets at all.

She wanted to be like him, with him.

Was it midnight yet? How could she tell? She looked up, trying to gauge the time from the sky: the legendary fairy punctuality had already slipped away from her.

As she reached the first rocks, the moon plunged into the sea, leaving only phosphorescent streaks on her stolen shift. Over there, at the end of the jetty, the light from the fire appeared to blaze more brightly. The boat wasn't so far away now. Underfoot, the stones felt hot and rounded. She leapt from rock to rock: a tiny white sail bounding over the scree of black pebbles, attracted by the glare of the lightship. For so many sailors on the open sea, this light had represented hope. She too was hoping to find her treasure, her shelter, her life there. But like all those other vessels before her, what she encountered was shipwreck.

* * *

She landed silently on the abandoned body. He was no longer breathing. His eyes gaped wide.

Like her, he must have been fifteen or sixteen.

He was laid out, alone, on the bridge of the boat.

"My love…"

She sighed with each breath, searching for a glimmer in his eyes. She let her weight press down on the boy's body, and cupped his face between her hands. Her heart against his, beating for two, aching for two. The boat creaked in the waves, but it didn't move.

"My love."

She whispered reproaches, prayers, eternal regrets as she nuzzled into his neck. She was clinging to his shoulders, rubbing her cheek against his hair.

Gradually, her breathing slowed and became more regular. She spoke less. The carpet of embers was several paces away, but the heat radiating from the copper-coated boat still reached them. She fell silent now. They must have been burning cedarwood, its fragrant incense rising up into the night. This peacefulness seemed to herald her own death.

Making a final effort to open her eyes, she saw a lamp swaying far off on the rocks. Someone was approaching. She tore herself away from this most painful of embraces and rolled into the shadows.

Several minutes went by. She clasped her hands together and wept in silence as she watched the man draw near.

At the end of the jetty was a long walkway. The boat was moored to a forest of stripped oaks, jutting out of the sea like columns. The old man stepped onto this walkway, which wound a course between the stakes. Every movement was slow. He dragged a straw sledge behind him, on top of which was a stretcher designed for emptying the ashes.

Watching him, she wondered whether he had been responsible for killing her love. Was he returning to dispose of the body?

He made it as far as the boy and appeared to be muttering something to him. From her position, huddled just behind them, she heard him say, "I will carry you now. Do not be afraid."

He manoeuvred the stretcher next to the body, and whispered again.

"You will wait inside the cliff…"

She hurled herself at the old man, knocking him over on the bridge. Quick as a flash, she grabbed the small axe from his belt. As he crumpled and groaned, she was already towering over him, holding the weapon to his forehead, ready to crack it like a nut.

The old man watched the girl in terror. Her face was like that of a wild animal, her small hand positioning the blade of the axe between his eyes.

"You killed him," she said.

He was staring at her: a vision of hair and shift all stiff with salt, and of cheeks and shoulders the colour of pink and white coral. Who was this girl, this ethereal force to be reckoned with, whose knees pinned him to the ground?

"No," he sighed, "I didn't kill him."

"Who did?"

The wind blew some escaped sparks from the blaze towards them.

"Nobody."

The axe rose up high.

"Taåg…"

Her hand froze.

"Taåg received the order to bring him here and kill him."

"Where is Taåg?"

"He has returned to his marshlands."

She gazed at the body on the other side of the straw sledge.

"He killed him…" she whispered.

"No."

She raised the axe high above the man's skull.

"I swear! No one. No one killed him."

The girl closed her eyes to avoid witnessing what her own arm was about to do, but the man spoke just in time.

"Taåg disobeyed the king."

She stopped again.

"He didn't kill him. I'm the only one who knows this. When my work is done, he will kill me."

"What work?"

"I must hide the body inside the cliff."

"Who killed him? Who?"

"Taåg did not wish to kill the son of a king."

"I know what he's like. Killing is second nature to him."

"He fears only the souls of kings."

"Who killed him?"

"That I cannot tell you," he said, weeping. "But I know that you will let me live. For nobody can answer you if I die."

Slowly, she lowered her weapon and let herself sink to the ground.

He was right. Only her own death could extinguish the question that consumed her.

She closed her eyes.

"Who is this young prince to you?" he asked softly.

She didn't answer. She was thinking about those winter mornings, when he would set off to swim in the misty lake, his skin steaming as he emerged from the water.

"He no longer inhabits this body," said the old man.

She opened her eyes again: had she heard him properly?

"The boy has been banished but, he is alive."

"Where?"

"Not here in the Kingdoms, but far away, in a place from which no one returns."

She stood up.

"What are you saying?"

"Taåg granted him exile to avoid killing him." He paused, before saying slowly, "Banishment by spell."

"Where? Where is he?"

"He no longer inhabits this body."

"Answer me!"

She brought the axe down onto the copper, fractionally above the man's face.

He sighed.

"In a time … a land…"

"Where?"

20

"Go. Or we will both die. Return to the forest. Taåg is coming back."

"What time? What land?"

"The young prince has been exiled to a place of no return. Taåg sent him to a land where no path, no sea can bring him back to us."

The wind had dropped by now, and the embers barely glimmered. She could feel the cold descending over her. A trembling seized her limbs.

The old man's last words made her stomach lurch.

"It would need the powers of a fairy to undo a spell such as this."

She stared at the ground to hide her tears. One by one, her powers were deserting her. She lay on her side, her helpless hands to her heart.

So she had lost everything: magic and love.

Slowly, she stood up and dragged herself the few paces towards the body of the exiled prince.

She leant over him. Had her beloved reached some faraway place? Where was he? Standing in some lost valley? Breathing in the night air in a land cut off from the Kingdoms?

She tried pleading one last time.

"Where has Taåg banished him to? Where?"

With the back of her hand, she stroked her beloved's

forehead, while the old man's voice answered from behind her.

"The young prince is in the one time, the one world where they don't believe in fairies or tales."

The sea had grown calmer all around. Only the gently foaming surf could be heard now and, in the distance, a horse galloping down the beach.

2

BETWEEN MY TEARS

FAR AWAY AND HALF A CENTURY LATER, IN A FOREST that was thick and deep all around me, I could see blood on the bark of a tree. I was fourteen, with a bag slung across my shoulder, wet hair in my eyes and no reason to be there.

I had set off, going straight ahead, to escape a broken heart. I had been walking for three hours, wherever the forest took me.

If I hadn't put my fingers on the tree, if I hadn't looked at my hands, perhaps nothing would have happened. Instead of getting lost, I would have found my way back to the bright strip of road a few kilometres off. I would have escaped the night.

But there on the palms of my hands, when I brought them closer to my face, I saw a red liquid, sticky as peach juice: it was blood, and it felt warm in the freezing air.

I wandered about through the dead leaves. It was still bright. The daylight cut through the sweet chestnut trees in shafts and spilled onto the moss. Five paces from there, I could see another large drop of blood when I bent down.

It was showing me the way.

I sensed that somewhere, between the trees, there was a wounded being that needed me.

"Who's there?"

My words were soft and faltering, spoken almost to myself. I stared at my hands: I was shivering again, having left without a coat, just this bag and nothing else, inconsolable. I had ditched my bicycle in the grass to leave the road, forget the girl and return to the wild.

Pretending to be in two minds about it, I let my hands fall to my sides. But I can vividly remember the sense of mystery that drew me towards the deepest part of the woods.

And so, like a wolf, I picked up the trail again. Each time, I had to bend over to see the drops materialize before my eyes, leading the way. On I pressed, pushing branches aside and trampling coils of brambles.

At times I sensed my sadness waning, as if the memory of the girl were struggling to keep up with me in the forest, the gentle sound of her breathing behind me growing more distant. I stopped to let her catch up, because it was too soon to abandon my grief. What was she called? She hadn't even told me her name. I threw back my head and roared at the sky.

If somebody had been in danger, they would have answered me. But I was met by silence. I'd pulled my hood up, and my bag was still over my shoulder. A few drops of rain splashed between the branches, landing around me. Never in my life had I shouted in a place where nobody could hear me. I felt a strange thrill mingling with my anxiety and tears. It was time to summon all my strength; the light was failing and I was far from everything.

Suddenly, between two fallen trees, I spotted a roebuck. He was staring at me, unflinching. I thought I had found the wounded animal I'd been pursuing, but his fur was as pure as the pages of a children's book, and his lower legs were almost white. Not a trace of blood. He seemed even more stunned than I was. A flurry of raindrops from a tree exploded onto the moss like a crystal ball. The roebuck took a step backwards. I could see the steam rising off his burning flanks. One blink of my eye, and he'd have vanished. I was thinking about the girl I'd wanted to hold in my arms, but who had fled a few hours earlier.

Finally, I took a step towards the animal and, as it disappeared, total darkness came crashing down on the woods.

The ground snapped underfoot as I tried to cover some distance. My hands groped from one tree to the next. I could no longer see the bloodstains that had been guiding me. I felt numb and I knew the cold was lying in ambush, waiting for me to stop so it could seize me by the neck. The night had done all it could to make me fall before it did. But I was still standing.

One more step, and a light appeared far ahead: a swaying patch of light; a square laid out on the ground in the darkness; a carpet of liquid gold. It moved. I closed my eyes. When I opened them again, the carpet was still there, and as I approached it, my feet sank into the ground.

At last I realized what was happening. Just in front of me was a wide river (I could hear it lapping) and that spot of light with golden panes in the water was the reflection from a lit-up window.

I picked up my bag with its treasure inside and hitched it back over my shoulder, before beginning to wade against the current with my hands held high. The strong undertow kept pushing me towards the left, but I resisted. Suddenly, the window went dark. I wanted to stay upright, so that I could assess the black shape looming on the opposite bank. Yes, there had to be a house over there in the dark, by the water's edge.

I hadn't forgotten the despair that had flung me into the woods in the first place. This sadness was becoming an ally, walking with me in the darkness. I was taming it.

The water, which was now up to my waist, was gurgling around me. I knew about the dangers of crossing unfamiliar rivers in the dark. My feet were sinking into the mud, and sometimes the current collided with my shoulder, attempting to knock me over. My response was to hold my bag high above my heard.

I thought I was safe. Surely I was over the halfway mark. But then I got pins and needles in my upper back, and my head started spinning. Something trickled down my forehead and into my eyes. The darkness began turning as well. What was happening? I braced myself in a bid to stay on my feet. My strength was ebbing from every pore. I was going to drown.

The window of light was reflected briefly again on the water. In my giddy state, I thought I could see a human pass before it, looking in my direction. I froze. Despite the cover of darkness, I was convinced that I'd been seen. I thought about the trail of blood in the woods. I wanted to turn back. But then I heard the sound of diving, three times, just ten metres away from me. The cold suddenly became unbearable. Seconds later, I saw a series of black shapes swimming across the square of light. Three animals were struggling against the current, their heads gliding on the surface. As I lost my balance, my bag briefly came into contact with the water, but I managed to grab hold of it just in time.

Those black shadows were heading towards me now, slicing through the waves. I tried to make for the bank I'd set out from, but my body had stopped responding.

When I finally managed to look round, the animals were no longer in the square of light; but I knew they had to be there, close by. I couldn't call out, and I imagined them to be muskrats, or bears or anacondas. I felt a body against my leg: one of the creatures had dived beneath me. The three animals all hurled themselves on their prey at the same time. They had me by the shoulders, and I was losing my footing as jaws slid over my body, albeit only biting into the canvas of my jacket. I felt myself being raised up. Then I lost consciousness.

My eyes flickered open, briefly, as enormous human

hands hauled me out of the water and onto a pontoon. I couldn't move at all.

Then I blacked out again.

I can remember being in a strange state, where shadows flitted in and out, together with night birds and the laughter of the girl who had made me dissapear from the world.

It was a busy, teeming dream in which I was trying to breathe and stay on the surface. A long, all-enveloping dream.

I didn't emerge from it until my body detected the gentle warmth of a fire nearby, the touch of linen sheets, the aroma of burnt pinecones. The idyll after the nightmare.

The silence whistled and crackled occasionally. I was sheltered, safe. It was raining outside. The leaden weight of the blankets was just as it should be. Half opening my eyes, I could glimpse, beyond the white curve of the pillow, one, two … *three* black dogs lying close to a fireplace. Where was their master, the giant who had rescued me from the water? I raised my hand to my forehead and felt a bandage.

"It was a branch from a bramble bush that wounded you…"

The voice came from the foot of my bed, high up, as if the giant's head were touching the beams. I couldn't make out his enormous body in the half-light.

"I used my nails to pull out every one of those thorns."

The warmth suddenly ceased to reassure me at all. I was picturing fingernails as long as sickles. How could I escape? I had heard that hostages always regretted those first minutes, when they still had a chance to get away. I tried to locate the door in the darkness. I would have to step over the dogs to reach it. One of them had woken up and was licking its paw.

"You must have been bleeding for several hours. My dogs pulled you out of the water just in time."

A pinecone blazed in the fire. With my head resting on the pillow, I saw the room light up. And the man became visible. He was perched on top of a ladder, and he was tidying some red and brown boxes. He didn't look like a giant or an ogre at all. He turned gently towards me.

Thinking about it now, I remember that his face seemed to have come from another world. But I was so distracted by what he said next that for a long time I forgot all about that first impression.

"You bled a great deal."

And as he said those words, I finally realized that the blood I had been following all along, the blood that had led me to this hearth, to these dogs and to this man, was my own blood. That was my discovery. Each time I had bent over, through my tears, a drop of blood had fallen from my forehead, and it had marked out a path.

The wounded beast I had been tracking was me.

3

THE REFUGE

I kept my eyes shut for a few minutes, trying to grasp what was happening to me. I could hear the scraping of the ladder at the foot of my bed. Let him think I was asleep. A plan was taking shape in my head, and I was waiting for the ideal opportunity.

Suddenly, without a sound, I sat bolt upright and slammed my feet onto the floor.

The drowsy dogs watched me dash for the door, try without success to open it, make my way back across the room whooping like a warrior, grab a poker for my weapon, drop it because it burnt my fingers, spin around, climb onto a table in combat position, open the window and throw myself outside.

The three dogs didn't move throughout this whole charade, and their master probably didn't even look up from what he was doing, while I had managed to twist my ankle, letting out another roar and landing face down in the grass.

Bravo. Some fights don't make for much of a spectacle.

So there I was, dragging myself along on my elbows. Since my tumble, I had covered all of one and a half metres in ten minutes. The rain was beating down more heavily now. I must have looked like an eel slithering through the damp grass. I could tell that I wouldn't make it much further, despite there being no crocodiles snapping at my shins, and no butcher's cleaver in my back. My departure had been met with total indifference.

It was the same reaction when I returned to the dry of the house. Dead calm. The man was sitting at his table, making notes in an open ledger. I managed to limp, sheepishly, as far as my bed. The dogs were asleep in a heap at their master's feet. He remained silent to begin with, absorbed in his work. I was shivering, and had pulled the blanket back over me.

"What was that? An escape?"

His head bent over his ledger, an invisible smile, not a hint of sarcasm in his voice. I felt all the more ashamed of my flight.

"Who are you?" I asked.

He screwed up his eyes, as if this were some vast

and unfathomable question; as if I had asked him whether God existed, or whether the universe had an edge somewhere, like a balcony you could lean over.

Then he looked at me for the first time, holding me in his stare.

Doubtless, there were four or five people like me hanging from his larder ceiling. For all I knew, he was planning to use my skull as a paperweight on his desk, and the small bones in my fingers to scoop out his snails at dinner, but somehow I no longer felt afraid. He had close-cropped white hair, a carpenter's smock and the slender hands of a seamstress. I guessed that he was about sixty. He was turning a pencil between his fingers, taking his time, concentrating hard. And when I looked into his grey eyes, it was like stepping onto a seashore in the rain.

I tried to resist his gaze. I kept telling myself that I mustn't fall asleep. I mustn't. I mustn't.

But that refrain, combined with my fatigue, made me drift off again.

The girl made the most of my dreams to launch a fresh assault.

She was about fourteen, so roughly the same age as me. In my sleep, she trampled on the pieces of me she had already broken. I could feel her bare feet on my body. It hurt, but I didn't push her away. I preferred this to the pain of her disappearing.

The next day, at dawn, it was no longer raining. The house felt deserted. A small patch of sunlight spread towards the bed. I scanned the room for the bag I'd arrived with. It had vanished. As I tested a foot on the floor, I discovered that I wasn't ready to leave yet. The pain was too acute for me even to take one step.

I sat on the mattress and began to look carefully around me. Until this point, I'd been so focused on the urge to escape, and concerned only with the exit and the enemy that I hadn't really taken anything in. But now that I had finally stopped, I was absorbing the extraordinary place in which I found myself.

It was a large square room, a bit smoky, with two windows. The oak ceiling was supported by posts. There wasn't much furniture: the table I had seen the previous day, a long counter with drawers, a few stools. On one section of wall, logs were piled up and held in place by large metallic rings. With this stockpile of wood rising to the ceiling, autumn and winter could have lasted for centuries. There was also an armchair that had seen better days, four bulbs hanging from the beams, a sink, a staircase, some baskets and an old bicycle propped up against a circular saw in the middle of the room, flaunting itself as if it were the height of stylishness. But it was what was behind me, close to the bed, which made the room look so peculiar.

The entire wall was lined from floor to ceiling with luggage. There were hundreds of suitcases piled high along the entire length of the room. They were all different, made of cardboard, leather and wood. They came in every shape and size, some with decorative hinges, some canvas, some shiny or matt; their colours ranging from red lacquer to saffron yellow, black ebony to ecru, along with dark browns, shades of tobacco and royal blue.

It looked like a sorting office in an old-fashioned railway station, with the smoke from the fireplace partially obscuring the mysterious wall just behind me.

"Are you off somewhere?"

The man who had just walked into the room didn't answer, but strode over to the table where he put down a bag.

My bag.

"What about you, then? What did you come here to find?"

I didn't know how to answer. I was running away from my sadness, but with what aim? In search of what comfort?

"Were you alone?"

"Yes."

"How old?"

"Fourteen."

"Won't someone be looking for you?"

"Who?"

He was standing with the sun behind him.

"Do you have a family?"

I had everything I could ask for on that front, the complete set in every size: but nobody at home would be looking for me. They thought I was away for the week. Since I didn't know what the man planned to do with me, I wasn't keen to reassure him.

"What about you? Do you have a family?"

Again, a dark cloud passed over his face, a chasm in which the answers floated light years away. The door swung open, letting in one of the wolfhounds.

The man began to lay out the contents of my bag on the table.

"What are you doing?"

I tried to stand up, but I'd forgotten about my injured ankle: it felt as if several rounds of ammunition were being emptied into my right foot. I fell back onto the bed.

"They're fragile. Don't touch them."

He picked out the objects very carefully, arranging them in a square.

On the table, there was now a flick-knife, a notebook, a camera, six films in their black and grey boxes and a small Super 8 movie camera, together with a brand new film.

"Leave them, they're mine."

He handled the camera first.

"I was going to throw all this in the mud," he remarked.

Another storm of bullets in my chest. The only traces I had left of the girl were rolled up tightly inside one of those films. A few undeveloped photos were my only treasure.

"I don't know why you came to my home with these things."

"I was lost. I didn't mean to come to your home."

"Is this yours?"

"Yes."

As it happened, the Super 8 belonged to my father, the camera to my mother, and I had taken the unused films from the chest of drawers in our sitting room. So, strictly speaking, none of it belonged to me, apart from the memories captured on the films. And I wasn't even sure that those memories were mine any more either.

The man had his back to me now. He seemed to be thinking.

Today, I understand all the threads of destiny that became knotted and intertwined in those few seconds. I have a clear view of what his story might have been, and mine too, if my bag had been flung into the mud. So why, when he had lived in fear of being tracked down for so many years, did he tweak that other thread, the thinnest one, the most fragile, the one that put him in danger? Why did he choose the most uncertain path?

He gave me back the camera.

How could he have guessed that this great risk, the risk of trust, would save him years later?

I think it was the cruel girl hidden in the spools who saved us both, by stealing a tear from me as he turned and saw me trying to hide my bloodshot eyes.

A few seconds later, he gathered up the objects and tossed the bag onto the bed, where it landed next to me.

"Don't use anything in that bag, for as long as you're in this house. Agreed?"

The door creaked and the two other dogs sloped in.

"Understood?"

"Yes."

4

THE GIRL

Almost to my annoyance, on the third evening I managed to walk as far as the fireplace. I was feeling in less of a hurry to recover. The house had ensnared me with its dark wood and tiles, like a cage that protected me from my sadness.

Leaning my shoulder against the wall, I contemplated the few steps I could scarcely believe I had taken. Beside me, the armchair was warming itself like an old toad by the fire. I didn't dare sit down; the flickering of the flames in its creases made it look like it was breathing. On the other side of the room, the wall of luggage also appeared to be alive. It had cast me under its spell from the very first.

The man's footsteps rang out on the wooden floorboards upstairs. I'd noticed that he only went up there occasionally, to swap a few mysterious suitcases and trunks or, late at night, to go to bed, because I was in the downstairs bed where he usually slept.

I was also dressed in his clothes, which I'd found laid out on my mattress the first morning. They were the kind of clothes I haven't worn since: a splendid pair of trousers, thicker than theatre curtains, a waistcoat in knitted black wool and socks to the knee.

My host treated me as if I were a guest of honour. From the first day, he never asked me when I intended to leave.

Outside in the dark, the dogs could be heard snorting as they emerged from the water. I felt at ease, standing there in the gloom. The windows were always covered with dark cloth as soon as night fell. No light could have been visible from the exterior.

I was trying to figure out this man's existence.

He lived hidden from the world, busying himself with perplexing tasks, working on his notebooks or immersed in his boxes and suitcases, ready to leave at any moment with his mountain of luggage. How had he come to be here? Through the window, I had watched him gathering the last vegetables of the autumn in the strip of kitchen garden between the water and the house. He roamed the woods for a few hours every day with a slingshot wrapped round his wrist. He would return home with a rabbit or birds, which the dogs carried.

Standing there, close to the fire, I noticed a small frame hanging from one of the posts that held up the ceiling. I made my way over to it like a tightrope walker, my injured ankle so precarious that I was afraid even a gust of air or a piece of grit might make me trip.

It was an old black and white photo of a strip of pavement and a shop window from a bygone era. The door was ajar. There was snow outside, and inside stood a man and a woman, presumably the shopkeepers. On their window, two words, sparkling like the sign of a jewellery shop, read:

ARTISANAL MARSHMALLOWS

And just below:

MAISON PEARL

This little confectionery shop, *Maison Pearl*, looked at once very simple and very sophisticated. Three boxes had been put out on the pavement, in the snow, awaiting delivery. In the bottom right-hand corner of the photo, somebody had written by hand:

Christmas soon. As you can see! Business is good.
The shop's doing well. Look after yourself.
Don't worry about us.

I could also make out a date written more clumsily, in different handwriting: *1941.*

I remember that this image changed the way I viewed the man and his house. A person who displays a photo of a sweet shop in his home can't be all bad. And the handwritten note reassured me. It was a sign from the outside world, correspondence between people, the words we write to share our news. That photo of *Maison Pearl* did me no end of good: it introduced a familiar note into the mystery that had kept me between those walls for nearly three days.

"You can walk?"

I hadn't heard the stairs creaking, but the man was already standing in front of the fire, staring at me.

"Was that your family?" I asked, pointing to the photo.

"In a way."

He was at risk of becoming talkative, and I wanted to make the most of it.

"What's in those suitcases?"

44

"Come here, so I can see you walking."

I took a few steps towards the fireplace. He was almost smiling.

"You see, she won't be the last to make you run through the forests."

"Who?"

I stared at him without understanding. He was amused and pushed me into the old armchair, where I landed softly.

"What did you say?"

"Nothing."

"About the girl who made me run … what did you just say?"

He crouched down in front of the fire, in the same position as when he was cooking. He made me two meals a day, which he pulled out of the flames like a blacksmith. But on that particular evening, he wasn't spit-roasting one of the little birds his dogs brought back for him and which he stuffed with ground chestnuts. He was simply watching the embers.

"Did I already tell you about the girl?" I asked.

"You're not to touch anything here. Understand?" he replied solemnly, trying to change the subject. "Don't open the suitcases."

"Have I talked to you about the girl?"

"No need."

"How d'you know, then?"

"I know nothing. I saw what state you were in."

He poked the fire with a branch, before adding, "I know. I've jumped from a moving train before, and it hurts rather less."

I couldn't follow half of what he was saying, but each word moved me. Yes, when I had left my bicycle in the grass to set off through the woods, I did feel as if I'd just fallen off a train.

I'd discovered that hidden behind the shock of first love was a bullet that shattered into a hundred pieces on impact, and it was called heartbreak. First love is a double-barrelled shotgun that doesn't forgive. That was what I had experienced just a few days earlier, and the earth was still trembling beneath my feet.

"I don't even know her name," I explained. "She didn't leave me with anything. You can't understand. Nobody can."

Still he didn't move. I'd just told him something I wouldn't have confided in my best friend or in my brothers. But without seeing his face, I realized that all this was familiar to him, that this pain had already touched his life.

He stared at his hands, which had spread before the

embers – pale hands, onto which the flames and all his memories were reflected.

"Tomorrow, I won't be around," he said. "I'll leave the dogs here, and I'll be back the day after tomorrow. Look after the fire, please."

He went up to bed without trying to prise any other secrets out of me.

A day and a night.

Never in my fourteen years had I been handed a blank page like this: freedom without limits, time entirely to myself. The gift of solitude, in a tiny kingdom at the water's edge, was all it took for the story world and real life to come swooping down on me. And from then on they would never let me go.

5

TREASURE

My first morning without him began with a fresh pang of sadness, just when I thought I was over it.

As I was putting on my own clothes again, the ones I'd arrived in and which were now clean and dry after being washed by my host, I found a blue feather in one of my trouser pockets.

I'd picked it up in the boat on the day I first met the girl. She'd worn it in her hair for three days. On the last evening, before her disappearance, I'd stolen it back from her, as if I'd had a premonition of what would happen.

Feeling the feather again in my pocket, between my fingers, I replayed those hours of my life in fast-rewind, from her vanishing to the moment when the girl had appeared for the first time in the water near the washhouse, framed by armfuls of reeds.

I took out the feather and held it to my nose, but it smelled of fresh soap now. I put it down in the middle of the table, turning over a glass to trap it, the way I used to with butterflies as a small child.

I sat down on the chair.

As I waited for my heart rate to steady, I looked around me at the room basking in the autumn sunlight. I found myself staring at the wall of luggage glistening with its secrets. From the outset, the mystery of this place had triggered a sort of pleasurable pain in me, a calling, an unfamiliar yearning to distract me from my misery.

By midday I was standing in the river, with water up to my knees, trying to catch freshwater crayfish. They stirred up the mud, producing clouds around me as I caught them with my fingers. I threw another three onto the pontoon before they could nip me.

Suddenly, I looked up.

Something had darted into the bushes, over on the other side of the water. The man wasn't due back with his boat until the following day. When I turned to look at the dogs lying on the grass, close to the house, they hadn't moved.

I carried on with my fishing, occasionally glancing

across to the far bank. I'd been crayfish collecting
from waterfalls before, with a whole group of cousins.
I remembered the creaking sounds of those black mon-
sters in the traps, and above all our joy, bare-chested,
in the freezing midsummer water. But all that belonged
to another life, before the boat, before the girl, before
she'd disappeared, abandoning me like a trap with a
hole in it. And as I recalled that other life, I couldn't
tell whether I missed it or not.

This time the noise came from higher up, in the
alder trees over by the house. A branch must have
fallen into the water. There was a beating of air, like
a duck taking off, except there was no duck. Ripples
spread outwards from the trees. One of the dogs had
stood up, interested in a crayfish that was trying to
make a getaway on the pontoon. I waded out of the
water and limped through the reeds.

I was astonished by how indifferent the dogs were.
In the normal scheme of things, they'd prick up an ear
at a lizard yawning a hundred metres off.

As I approached the alders, I grabbed a stick to
poke around in the roots that sank deep into the water.
I glanced around me, feeling anxious for the first time,
before heading back towards the pontoon. Most of the
crayfish hadn't waited for me. I put the last two in a

bowl meant for bailing out the boat when it rained.

That's when I think I saw her.

A sort of golden light spread itself around me, and I turned to face one of the windows, guessing that it had to be the reflection of the sun on the glass. I saw a figure go past, behind the window. My heart felt like bursting. Despite such a brief appearance, I was sure I had recognized the girl.

I rushed barefoot towards the house. I couldn't even feel my battered ankle any more. The dogs followed, concerned about what was happening to me. As I pushed open the door, I was struck by how dark it was inside.

"Who's there?" My eyes were slowly becoming accustomed to the gloom.

I turned around and saw that the place was deserted. Nobody. Not even the dogs had followed me.

I strained my ears for the sound of footsteps or squeaky floorboards upstairs. Nothing.

"I saw you. I know you're here."

I paced back and forth over by the windows, and searched again under the stairs.

"Tell me where you are."

A dog was rubbing itself against my damp legs, trying to calm me by purring like a cat. I kicked him away.

I must have looked like a madman when I finally stopped in the middle of the room, barefoot, my rolled-up trousers dripping onto the floor and my lips quivering.

"Answer me."

I should have remembered not to leave those walls, not even for a few crayfish. I knew that my broken heart was waiting for me at the door, hidden in the reeds.

I was alone in the world, and I began to cry like a small boy lost in a crowd. My voice grew weaker. I pressed my forehead against one of the wooden posts.

"At least tell me your name..."

Several minutes went by before I could accept that grief had led me astray, and that if I carried on like this I would lose my mind. I had to leave. No time to wait for the man's return.

If I steered a straight course, then once I'd made it to the other side of the river and walked through the woods for a few hours, I'd be bound to find my bicycle, or a road at any rate. There'd be cars, people, proper things to dream about, and perhaps more girls, dozens of girls, one of whom would, miraculously, accept all the feathers I collected for her and wear them in her hair.

So I sat down on the bed to put my shoes on. The

dogs frolicked around me, delighted that I had calmed down. But their cheery mood was forced and unnatural, like that of dogs who have just witnessed their master crying.

I crossed the room to pick up my jacket, which was hanging by its hood from a nail and glanced one last time at the photo of *Maison Pearl*. Then I walked back again to pick up my bag. There was nothing missing: the camera, the Super 8 and the rest of my belongings were all inside. I was ready.

But when I turned to face the wall of suitcases, I spotted something I hadn't noticed before. In the midst of all that piled-up luggage, that mound of leather, canvas, handles and locks, one suitcase was wide open, propped on top of two other. There it was, gaping like a shellfish. How had I not noticed it when I'd woken up that morning? How had it opened?

I went over to get a closer look. Inside were lots of tiny white paper packages, neatly arranged.

For the first time, one of the dogs growled. I took another step and then stopped. I had made for the suitcase with the idea of closing it again, but the growling of the first dog, and the position of the other two, stationary, ready to pounce, pricked my curiosity.

Gently, I led the dogs outside.

53

"There you go… Guard the house."

Once I'd closed the door, I could hear them scratching on the doorstep.

Alone again inside, I glanced at the windows. The dogs would alert me of the man's return. I had nothing to fear.

The white paper packages were of different shapes and sizes, ranging from tiny to considerably larger. A well-wrapped rectangle filled almost half the suitcase. There must have been plenty more below it. Thousands, if all the suitcases were full. I was already wiping my fingertips on my jacket. How could I resist?

I opened the first parcel by choosing the smallest of all, as if that would make my crime less serious. The paper used to wrap the objects was always the same: printed white tissue paper of the finest quality. I was frightened of crumpling it and leaving tell tale marks.

The first object was a thimble in a red box. I turned it over between my fingers, while holding the box in my other hand. I'd played with the old thimbles in my grandmother's chest of drawers, at her apartment on Avenue Mozart in Paris, but none were as chiselled or refined as this. Holding it up to my eyes, I could see that it was made of a gilded metal. A carved band spiralled downwards dozens of times like an irregular garland finer than a hair, encircling the thimble, which just fitted onto my little finger.

When I opened a second parcel, I discovered a marble the size of a shooter, made from orange-coloured glass, which looked like a sunset in a hurricane. In the centre was an apple pip. The marble was in a silver mount, so that it could be worn as a piece of jewellery.

I then unwrapped another pendant: a tiny ivory skull with dark, hollow eyes. And after that, in three layers of paper, a little nightshirt embroidered with pearls, white and frothy as gossamer.

My heart was pounding. The objects were laid out in front of me on the white paper. No doubt about it. It had all become clear: the isolated house, the dogs, the black drapes over the windows at night. I was in a brigand's cave. The man went out plundering museums and castles, then stockpiled his booty here.

Drunk with the sense of danger, I began to open the large rectangle wedged into the right-hand side of the suitcase. I had just noticed that the white paper on all the packages was printed with the name of the shop in the black and white photo: *Artisanal Marshmallows, Maison Pearl*. The burglar's treasure was masked by that deceptive wrapping, like a giant emerald concealed in a sweet wrapper.

The fourth object didn't look like a collector's item. It was a scrap of wickerwork that must have come from a piece of furniture, and it muddied my explanation. Unless it was a strip torn from a toy box belonging to Cleopatra or Napoleon, I couldn't see how it had any value whatsoever.

How could I have guessed then that it was the most prized possession in the man's treasure trove? That little scrap of willow, the remains of a cradle, became covered in buds each spring to attract the birds, and the man never held it in his hands without weeping.

I wrapped each of the objects again and put them back in the suitcase, closing it carefully. It was time to leave. With my bag on my shoulder, I pushed open the door. The dogs licked my hands and watched me go, without reacting, as if they didn't believe I was serious.

They were right. As I stepped back into the river, I heard the same rustling as earlier, but this time at water level. The beating of a heart or a wing, the slap of a wet skirt? Closing my eyes, I managed to resist the downward spiral that was boring into me again. But I couldn't help thinking of the girl's blue feather: I had left it under its glass cover in the house.

I retraced my steps, happy at the excuse to return. The house welcomed me back with its lingering haze of burnt pinecones, and that coppery light on the suitcases. It was as though it were putting on a show to keep me under its spell.

I made my way over to the table and lifted up the glass.

The feather was gone.

6

SMALL GHOSTS

He found me asleep at ten the next morning, lying fully clothed on the bed. I didn't dare move.

I must have collapsed, exhausted, at daybreak.

With my head resting on the pillow, I listened to the sound of his footsteps on the beaten earth floor. I was afraid. Did he know what I'd been up to all night? He was coaxing the fire back to life. When the kettle began to whistle, I turned my head very gently and saw that he wasn't watching me. He had arrived with a new suitcase, which he'd left by the door.

My plan had been to escape before his return, but sleep had got the better of me before I'd finished my work. I scanned the room. The other suitcases were all in their places and, magically, the camera seemed to have been tidied away into its bag at the foot of the bed.

I couldn't remember how the night had ended. But the

mystery of the disappearing feather had set everything off.

To begin with, I'd spent an hour spread-eagled on the bed, gathering my thoughts. Then, I'd taken out my camera like a handgun from its holster.

I had a premonition: if blue feathers and girls could disappear without leaving any trace, then everything else might vanish too, as soon as I crossed the river. The house, the man, the suitcases and their contents, the pear trees leaning on the wall, the crayfish and the black dogs: all of it could evaporate into thin air. I was surrounded by small ghosts that unsettled me, creaking their pinchers or rustling their skirts by the water's edge.

And so I had broken all the rules, spending the rest of the afternoon and all night long photographing the house and its treasures.

For a year now, a weapon that showed no mercy had taught me how to hunt down ghosts and pin them to the walls. I had found happiness in my father's darkroom: a cupboard lit by a red bulb, where all the light in the world appeared on the paper you dipped into transparent baths. I could lock myself in there for hours on end.

It was this sudden passion that had led me to the depths of the countryside. My parents had let me sign up for a course during the school holidays.

The advert, torn from a bakery window, read:

Enter the world of photos!
A week in autumn
to learn all about photography.

I still have a vivid recollection of the drawing underneath: a hen perched on a camera.

Every evening, in my bed, I kept turning that strip of paper – no bigger than a metro ticket – over in my hand. The hen seemed to be challenging me.

The first day of the holidays, I was escorted to the Gare Montparnasse together with all sorts of tips and a ham sandwich. I caught three different trains, each slower and noisier than the last, before arriving into what appeared to be the smallest station in western Europe.

I got off at the same time as two postal bags, which were thrown onto the platform. A man welcomed me, his cap tucked under one arm. He looked like the stationmaster, but turned out to be the postman.

While I was looking for someone else on the deserted platform, he said my name.

"Yes, that's me."

"I was expecting you."

I put my bicycle in the back of his yellow van, then sat in the passenger seat. Once we were on our way, the postman explained to me that he handled the transport side of things since Rachel didn't have a car.

"Thank you," I said, not knowing what else to say.

But I had no idea who Rachel was.

The van passed through marshland covered with bushy green lentil plants, where small bridges straddled the various channels beneath a grey sky.

"In exchange," he said, "she gives me eggs."

The road had just entered a forest of russet hues.

"Eggs?"

He didn't answer. I was thinking back to the hen on the advert, when he stopped in front of a farm.

"There you go. It's here."

I was still confused about the eggs.

"See you next Sunday," he said, waiting for me to get out of the van.

"See you Sunday."

I pulled out my bicycle, which was buried under his postal bags.

The farm looked like a giant henhouse at the edge of the forest.

I pushed my bicycle into the courtyard, slaloming between the columns of chicks standing guard. The mistress of the house was indeed called Rachel, and my arrival seemed to take her by surprise.

I quickly realized I was the only person who had signed up for the course and that if, by some chance, Rachel had ever been involved in photography, it was in a former life. There was no hint of a camera or a photo lab in this house.

She cooked me an omelette. Then she showed me to the bunk beds in a small grey wooden building.

"See you tomorrow."

In the middle of the night, I switched on my torch to read the advert again:

Enter the world of photos!

Across the yard, Rachel was listening to music.

I fell back to sleep.

"You'll spend the first three days looking for your subject."

"My subject?"

It was grey outside, still almost dark. Rachel was pouring me a glass of milk, head bent so as not to spill any. The lenses on her glasses were as thick as ice cubes.

"Go for a walk. Look around you. Find your subject. Got it?"

"Got it."

And for three days, I followed her advice. I would set off in the morning with my bicycle and my hard-boiled eggs. I was back by the evening, when we'd eat an omelette under the flickering strip-light.

My search was over on the morning of the fourth day, when the girl appeared on a boat.

I had found my subject. My subject was pushing her boat with a three-metre pole. My subject moved about barefoot and on tiptoes in her boat, cutting willow branches to make into bundles.

On the afternoon of the sixth day, my subject flew away. The girl had disappeared. I found a telephone box on the side of the road and called Rachel, informing her in a flat voice that I had to go back home because my grandmother was poorly. She seemed rather relieved by the bad news.

"What about getting to the station? Would you like me to call the postman?"

I was holding back my sobs by gagging my mouth with my right hand.

"I've got my bicycle."

"Sorry?"

"My bicycle."

In fact, my bicycle was lying in a grassy ditch.

She hung up. I made my way back to the forest with a broken heart.

Five days later, there I was lying on that bed, trying not to attract any attention.

"I saw the crayfish outside," the man said abruptly.

Through the gloom, he must have noticed that my eyes were open. Was it possible that my crime had gone undetected? He was talking as if he hadn't been away at all.

"Yes, I caught them yesterday," I said, stretching. "Where did you go?"

"I don't travel very far any more."

He brought me a cup of hot water that carried the scent of vanilla. I propped myself up on the pillows and held out my hand, then clasped the cup hastily.

"It's hot," he pointed out.

"I'll be fine," I said, scalding my fingers rather than letting him notice anything: my palm was covered with the lists I'd copied out during the night.

Each of the packages in those suitcases had a three

or four-figure number written on the bottom of it; presumably so that the man could identify the objects listed in his ledgers. I'd picked out a few at random, trying to grasp the meaning of his collection.

He moved away from me.

Over on the other side of the room, the ledgers that represented the missing part of my investigation were stacked against the window.

Everything I'd seen in the suitcases the previous night had made me reel between wonder and confusion. I had no idea whether this man was a highwayman, a rag-and-bone man, a madman or a poet. The key to the mystery surely lay in those notebooks, which I had yet to open.

"I've been meaning to tell you," he mumbled. "I was thinking things over, on the train."

Aha! So he'd taken the train.

When I'd first spotted his new suitcase, I'd assumed that all I needed to do was search the newspapers for records of burglaries that had taken place in the region during the preceding days. But in twenty-four hours, and on a return train ticket, he could have crossed borders. He could have stolen the Crown Jewels from London, Brussels or Madrid. Then again, was there any point in trying to find out? He was just as likely to

THE BOOK OF PEARL

have brought back a rusty old nail in a velvet pouch.

"I was thinking about something…"

The dogs blinked drowsily with each sound that escaped their master's lips. My guess was that they only heard his voice on rare occasions.

"Something that I need to talk to you about…"

"Yes."

"It's time for you to go, now."

"Why?"

"I told you that I know all about it. What you're experiencing. The girl. I said that, didn't I?"

"Yes."

"So you must go, if you are to leave her behind you."

"Leave who?"

It was at that moment I finally noticed his accent and the unusual pattern of his sentences. He was trying to get a word out, but it was stuck in his throat.

He tried again.

"Sadness."

But I already knew what he meant.

"It's something that can fill one's life. Turning round and round inside you, until you die."

Now he had my attention.

"But if you're able to leave your sadness behind you in the grass, then that is what you must do. Keep it hidden in the grass. Gently explain to it that you want something else, that you bear nothing against it, but that you're off."

I was imagining a small animal, crouching in a meadow, and the sound of footsteps getting fainter, as the long grass was trampled underfoot.

"What about you? What do you do with it?"

He walked towards me, smiling, his eyes lowered.

"With what?"

"Sadness."

"I am no example."

"Neither am I."

"But you…"

He trailed off, before admitting, "My sadness is all that I have left, if I am to return to where I come from."

"Where you come from?"

And these are the words he said – I can still hear them, twenty-six years on.

"I must keep my grief alive."

The dogs went over to lavish him with their affection in his moment of sorrow.

"Where *is* the place you come from?"

"Gather your belongings. I'll be waiting for you on the pontoon."

He went outside with his small pack of wolfhounds.

I walked to the window and watched him go over to the boat. Then I picked up one of the large ledgers and opened it at the first page.

There were four words written in black ink:

JOSHUA PEARL, VOLUME SEVEN

And below:

FROM 345 TO 487

I quickly checked the numbers on my hand. Only one number corresponded with the ledger.

I leant towards the window to keep an eye out. Pearl was still there, crouched on the pontoon. I ran to fetch my bag from the foot of the bed and quickly removed the camera. Without losing a second, I photographed the first page, hoping that the morning light would be strong enough. But I was at the end of the film. I rewound, using the little handle underneath the main body of the camera.

Outside, Pearl was watching one of his dogs swimming. I took out a new film, tossing the other one back into my bag. The camera was ready to go again in a matter of seconds.

I turned the pages of the notebook frantically, sliding

my fingers down the numbers in the left-hand margin.

410, 430, 460...

461.

I looked up. One of the dogs was climbing back up onto the bank, a live moorhen in its jaws. There was nobody on the pontoon now. My god.

I put the open ledger down, no time to read it, and took a step backwards with the viewfinder to my eye. The white frame was blurry. Once everything was in focus, I pressed down on the shutter release.

There was a hand on my arm.

I have no memory of what happened next.

Only that I woke up by the roadside, at nightfall, with my bicycle next to me in the long grass.

7

THE CASTAWAY

Wrapping strips of marshmallow is a tricky business.

They have a gooey, slippery consistency and, despite the icing sugar that's meant to stop them from sticking, more often than not Jacques Pearl felt as though he spent his days slopping noodles into tissue paper.

The customer watched him at work, her eyes agog. She was wearing a hat adorned with a bow on one side, a coat with a bow at the back, and low-heeled shoes each with a large bow on top. There was a silk scarf knotted to her handbag, too.

This was clearly a lady who knew a thing or two about wrapping.

The year was 1936. It had been raining solidly for two days, and the night before, Paris had witnessed its worst storm in twenty years, fiercer even than the bombings of the Great War.

Pearl slid a ridged sheet of card onto the tissue paper, then heaped a pound of marshmallows on top, their square ends immaculately arranged like a chessboard. He cast a fleeting glance through the window to the pavement opposite.

The boy was still there, standing on the cobblestones in the rain.

Pearl started folding.

"What are the black ones?"

"They're blackberry, madame."

"Right then, swap me a white one for a black one."

He obliged with a smile. At *Maison Pearl*, the customer was king. Hence the pearl-studded crown that had served as the shop's emblem for half a century.

Reopening the patterned tissue paper and replacing an almond marshmallow with a blackberry one, Pearl asked, "Do any of the other flavours take your fancy?"

He was all too familiar with customers who dithered, and liked to nip any indecision in the bud.

"No. Hurry up. My husband's waiting in his automobile."

Pearl placed a fresh piece of tissue paper underneath the card so that there wouldn't be a crinkle in sight. He glanced across the street again and resumed folding the paper over the marshmallows.

"And the orange ones?"

"I showed you those a second ago. The orange ones are orange."

"You don't say!" said the lady, as if she were being taken for a fool. "So, give me half an orange one."

"I'm sorry, madame, but I don't cut the marshmallows."

"And why not?"

"We have never cut the marshmallows at *Maison Pearl*."

The lady seemed vexed by this news.

"Now listen here..."

Pearl interrupted his wrapping once again.

"Since when have you not cut them?"

"Let me see... We haven't cut our marshmallows for forty-eight years. Or is it forty-nine? We're in 1936 now, and my mother established the shop in 1888, after the death of my father, Abel Pearl."

"Is that really a proper French name?"

"I beg your pardon?"

"Do me a whole orange marshmallow, then, since you refuse to go to the effort..."

"With pleasure."

Once again he changed the tissue paper, took his silver tongs and picked up an orange marshmallow, sending a flurry of citrus flavours across the room.

"Actually, no," she sighed. "Put that one back. My husband's expecting me. This is all taking too long, and I'll get plump."

The husband, the waiting, the waistline ... Pearl listened to all these excuses with a tinge of weariness. He laid down the marshmallow and the tongs, and continued with his folding.

"Dear me, it's not very busy in here, is it?" she tutted, surveying the deserted shop.

It occurred to Jacques Pearl that this lady's guts might be a good substitute for the gelatine in his next batch of marshmallows.

"The shop would usually have closed twenty-five minutes ago," he said, without raising his voice. "It's seven o'clock in the evening. I've sold twenty-seven kilos of marshmallows since this morning, despite the storm of the century. They were queuing outside in the rain as far as the hotel. No, madame, business is not doing badly at all."

"Are you losing your temper?"

But Pearl didn't even hear the question. His eyes were back on the drenched boy standing under the gutter with water cascading onto him, his feet in the torrent of the street.

"Because if you are, I shall call for my husband who's waiting in his automobile at the corner of the square."

"I won't let him die in the cold and the rain."

"My husband?!"

"I have to get him away from there."

"Are you … talking about my husband?"

Pearl abandoned the package and the lady, skirted round the counter and headed for the door, grabbing an umbrella as he went. The customer was quick to brandish her own.

"Leave him alone!"

Pearl was already outside. He opened the umbrella and crossed the road.

The boy was maybe fifteen or sixteen. He was standing bolt upright in his dripping clothes, his entire body shivering as he gazed at the shop's emblem.

"What are you doing here, my young friend?"

He didn't answer, or even seem to understand, but his eyes were glued on Jacques Pearl, as if he were establishing whether or not he had cause to be afraid.

"Come with me."

Pearl covered him from the rain and led him away.

They bumped into the lady, who was running through the rain with her marshmallows.

"You're all the same!" she said, looking at Pearl.

The wind suddenly flipped her pink umbrella inside out so it looked like a flaming torch. She let out a cry and started gesticulating madly at an oncoming car. Pearl left her marooned in the middle of the road, spluttering fit to drown.

The boy was soon sitting on a chair in the shop with a bath-towel draped round his shoulders. Jacques Pearl had lowered the iron shutter and was covering the marshmallow display shelves with a white gauze, as though he were tucking in his children for the night.

"I'm in a bit of a quandary, here..."

But despite his misgivings, Pearl's excitement was palpable.

"My wife went up an hour ago. She's waiting for me. What will she say if I turn up with you? Where on earth have you appeared from?"

But he didn't seem overly worried about his wife's reaction, as he started turning out the lights.

"Try to say something to me, my young friend. Your name. Anything. What were you doing out there in the storm?"

The boy said nothing. He'd stopped shivering. He stared straight into the filament of the light bulb above him, then watched Pearl as he performed his duties with precise, economic movements. Whether closing the door of the wood-burner, stowing the scissors into a drawer, passing a cloth over a dusting of sugar, or turning the key in the cash register, each motion was a glimpse of perfection. The boy was also studying the *Maison Pearl* emblem on the window.

Pearl stopped suddenly.

"Español?"

For the past several months, young refugees had started crossing the Pyrenees because of the Spanish civil war. The French authorities were keeping a very close watch on them. But this boy didn't seem to know that Spain even existed.

Pearl removed his apron without taking his eyes off the new arrival, and hung it behind the counter.

"I hope my wife won't disapprove too much," he fretted, but there was a smile playing across his face.

Madame Pearl greeted them with loud shrieking. How could he have left the boy for so long in a sopping wet shirt? She unbuttoned it as if he were a five year old and rushed to fetch him some dry clothes. In a small bedroom at the end of the hallway, there was a wardrobe full of their son's belongings.

Jacques Pearl dressed their unexpected guest in the

bathroom. Despite the collection of combs lined up below the mirror, he was unable to tame the boy's wild locks.

Pearl brought him into the kitchen looking as pale and handsome as a young bridegroom. A third place had already been laid at the table, and Madame Pearl was busy topping up the soup tureen from a large stock-pot. Just next to it, potatoes were whistling away in some butter. Madame Pearl filled up half the room, but she billowed around with such ease that it was as if the varnished wood table lifted to make way for her, while the bottles and pepper mill moved aside for her blouse.

Standing by the window, the boy was swaying too, overwhelmed by such gentleness, by such warmth, and by the scent of the waxed wooden floor.

That evening, they settled him into their son's bedroom.

The Pearls didn't even try to fall asleep. Holding hands in bed, they lay on their backs and listened to the boy tossing and turning down the hallway.

They had left all the doors open to hear this other presence in their home.

"Tomorrow, we'll decide what's to be done," said Jacques Pearl.

"Tomorrow, yes."

But they were in no hurry for tomorrow to come.

The boy was exactly the same age that Joshua, their only son, had been when he had died two years earlier.

"I have to say, his hands don't look like a vagabond's," said Madame Pearl, suddenly an expert in the matter.

"No."

"Listen."

They could hear a creak of the floorboards.

As Jacques Pearl got out of bed, he felt a gust of cool air blowing down the hallway. The boy had opened the window and was watching the rain. He held one hand outside, cupping it to drink from the sky, while with the other hand he clasped a red blanket around his neck, which trailed behind him like the train of a young king.

Without making a sound, Pearl fetched a jug and a glass, which he placed next to the bed. The boy turned round.

The next day, Jacques Pearl sat him on a stool behind the counter. He left his wife to hold the fort, then took Rue du Temple and snaked down to the Seine, crossing Île de la Cité before heading up Boulevard Saint-Michel and knocking at the door of the asylum for the deaf and dumb. The idea had come to him as he studied the boy closely over breakfast. Perhaps he had escaped from an institution of this sort.

Pearl stepped through the doorway and asked the gatekeeper if he'd had any news of a runaway.

"Why? Have you found someone?"

"No, no. Definitely not. But in this weather, I can't help thinking that nobody ought to be outside long. Are you missing anyone?"

"What age?"

"Fifteen or sixteen? I... I'm just plucking a number out of thin air. Just a hypothesis."

"A what?"

"A hypothesis."

The gatekeeper recoiled as if this were some kind of contagious disease, like hepatitis or pneumonia.

"If, by some misfortune," Pearl elaborated, "a boy of fifteen were to end up on the streets in this weather..."

The gatekeeper smoothed his moustache with a finger.

"No. All of our children are here, and in good health."

"That's just as well. Good day."

Feeling relieved, Pearl was already heading for the door. The man's footsteps pattered after him down the hall.

"Monsieur!"

He turned round.

"If you've found a fifteen-year-old boy, you'd do well to take him to the police."

"I haven't found anyone. Thank you for your time."

He withdrew rapidly into the street, just a stone's throw from the Jardin du Luxembourg, as the sun was rising.

On returning to his shop, Pearl saw that the customers were paying no attention to the boy in the corner sticking labels onto paper bags. He was applying himself well. Every now and then, Madame Pearl would glance over at him protectively, and when she saw her husband walk in, she jabbed an inquisitive chin at him. Pearl shook his head slightly to indicate there'd been no news. Their eyes met, glowing with joy.

Having taken this single measure, Pearl decided that he had done all he could to unravel the mystery. Quite frankly, what more could he think of? Going to the police? He refused to entertain the idea for a second. And if someone had misplaced the boy, they only needed to come and ask for him back.

This is how a stranger who had appeared out of the blue, a passenger in the storm, came to enter the Pearls' home without anyone really noticing. He became known as "our young friend", "the boy" or "the Spaniard". Before long he proved himself indispensable. He worked hard in the shop, handling enough chores for three assistants. And when, thanks to two years of evening classes in Madame Pearl's dining room, he learnt to speak French, it also became clear that, beneath his melancholy, he was intelligent, lively and charming, this grey-eyed boy with the faint, unplaceable accent.

8

THE OPENING

Some of the girls were in love with him. One, whose name was Rosa, came every evening throughout the summer of 1938. He walked with her for an hour after closing time, escorting her back to the Passage du Prado where her father had a barbershop. On his return to *Maison Pearl*, he knew that the shop would be dark, with Madame Pearl spying on him from the first floor. He would head upstairs. The door was always left open, and the refrain from the kitchen would be the same, "Well, my boy?"

He'd come and sit next to her while she peeled the potatoes or filleted some fish. She never let him help, but just looked at him with a knowing expression full of nudges and winks. He would keep both his hands under the table like a good boy.

"Did you go for a walk?"

He would nod.

"That's nice. And you didn't feel like taking her to the cinema?"

"No."

Madame Pearl knew that going to the cinema usually helped move things along.

"Do you chat together?"

"A bit."

"She's very pretty."

He'd nod some more.

"There's that other girl from the café who passed by the shop. What was her name again?"

"Adrienne."

"Ah, will you listen to that: Aaaaaadrienne…"

She started laughing.

"I can see why they're falling like flies. What is that accent of yours? One day you'll tell me, won't you, my dark horse?"

Sometimes, by accident, Madame Pearl would hear him speak in his language. It made her tremble all night long.

For there were days of fever, too. Days when the boy was unrecognizable. He would turn his room upside down and roar at the window, then thrash against Jacques

Pearl, who'd try to block him as he hurtled down the stairs before disappearing for three or four days at a time. Madame Pearl called these his "frenzies".

They were violent, his frenzies. All the walls of the building would shudder, right down to the cellar.

He was like a soul possessed, railing at the sky and sinking his nails into his pillow. He spoke of getting away from there, of escaping this world. In a whirlwind of feathers, he would utter sentences in his language that sounded like groans of agony, or like the howl of a wolf trapped in a snare. He would open the wardrobes and pound at the back of them with a chair leg, as if he wanted to reach the other side. He spoke of forgotten paths, of passages. When his cries had faded into the night, Madame Pearl would stay behind to sweep up the shattered plates on the kitchen floor. She would hand out mountains of sweets to the neighbours to beg their forgiveness, before opening up the shop.

A few days later, they would come down at dawn to discover the boy moulding strips of marshmallow in the back room, where the scent of violet filled the air.

"All well, our young friend?"

He'd lift his head in greeting, and his eyes would appear to have found a modicum of peace for the next few weeks. No one knew where he went during those episodes. But his meek presence, hard-working hands and far-reaching expression meant that people didn't dwell on his frenzies for long.

Every year, on Christmas Eve, *Maison Pearl* opened its doors to the children. They came galloping down the street like marauding barbarians, straight from school with their satchels in tow. They stopped at the door, gasping for breath, smoothing their hair as they gazed through the window. Then they would enter, one by one, taking care not to barge, their angelic faces and streaming noses buried in their scarves. The older girls, no longer eligible for this ritual, would hold hands with the younger ones to play down their age. The good children tried to behave even better, remembering to say, "Good morning" and "Merry Christmas". Even the naughty ones, their caps bunched up in their hands, were mesmerised by the orderliness, the golden glow of the light, the copper containers and the sense of walking through a cloud of icing sugar. They would tug at their shorts to hide their knees that were muddy from games of marbles in the dirt.

Each of them received a marshmallow that had been wrapped up in specially printed red-and-white paper.

On Christmas Eve, the children were allowed ahead of the throng of customers in the shop. Once they'd been served, they dawdled a bit, too happy to leave. Each step was in slow motion. Not a single one of them, however, would dare queue up a second time – that would risk being condemned to "seven years". This was the threat that Monsieur Pearl would issue each and every time: seven years without Christmas marshmallows if you were caught cheating. When you're only six or eight, seven years seems a lifetime.

But back in that winter of 1938, as Paris's Jewish quarter teemed with small businesses and artisanal shops, it was better to possess no power of imagination. Who could bear to contemplate the fates of those young faces seven years later, when the war would be over and they would be entitled to their mashmallows once again?

As soon as the crowd had dispersed and the iron shutter had been half-lowered, the boy sent Monsieur and Madame Pearl upstairs.

"I'll close up. You go and sleep."

Jacques Pearl didn't put up much resistance. He could see how tired his wife was, and he was so rattled from the day's events that he himself could barely stand.

That very morning, two gendarmes had arrived from the police station amid the rush of customers and children. Pearl had shown them into the back room.

They had come in search of a certain Joshua Pearl, whom they accused of failing to report for military service. Pearl let them speak, his jaw clenched, before telling them that his son had never been that sort of boy, and that he would have been first in line to serve his country.

"The first, you hear me?" he said, before adding, "If he hadn't died five years ago."

Pearl would have maintained his wounded dignity had it not been for one of the gendarmes, who buried his nose in his report and asked, "Are you sure about that?"

And so the father was forced to recall the shape of his son's body, draped in a sheet in the sitting room. The look on Jacques Pearl's face told the gendarmes that they'd be well advised to leave.

It was now eight o'clock in the evening, and Jacques Pearl's heart still hadn't recovered its normal rhythm. The confectioner took his wife's arm and turned to the young man.

"Thank you for closing up, my boy. When you're done, there's a Christmas party at the plasterer's on

Rue de Saintonge. His three daughters passed by yesterday, one after the other, to invite you. Go and enjoy yourself."

The Pearls each gave their boy a peck on the forehead before retiring upstairs. They made a point of not celebrating Christmas, as a mark of respect to their own religion.

So the young man stayed by himself and meticulously cleaned the display cases. After the great invasion, there wasn't a single marshmallow left in the establishment. Tomorrow would be the one day of the year when *Maison Pearl* kept its doors closed.

Slowly he swept the shop floor feeling a warm sense of well-being. The fire in the wood-burner was out but the stove was still giving off some heat. At the foot of the velvet curtain that protected against the draught, he saw something poking out. It was a book, with a slightly scuffed cover.

He picked it up and wiped it on the curtain.

It was an illustrated book that a child must have dropped while waiting in line for marshmallows.

There were no books in the Pearls' house. Only an enormous dictionary with a lock, which was kept in the glass cabinet in the sitting room, just in case. But there was no other book in sight. Jacques and Esther

Pearl read the newspapers every day to keep up with what was happening in the world. And if their dead son did once have a handful of children's books, they had long since been given away to good causes in the area.

The boy gazed for a moment at the red and gold cover, not daring to open it. He went to lay the book on the counter.

There was one more large vat to be rinsed out, which he carried through to the sink in the back room. He turned the tap to fill it up and, as the water was running, made his way back to the counter.

To keep his hands busy, he put the pencils back in their pot and scratched a small bit of sugar from the metal edge, before pulling the book towards him and opening it.

He leant forward to read the first line his finger had landed on.

Reading was a struggle for him, and he was still very slow, but eventually, one by one, the words leapt from the page.

He looked up in a state of agitation, rushed to turn off the water that was already overflowing, and returned to the book. He found the sentence that he'd read before and started from the beginning. It was still there. And even if he closed his eyes, there it was when he opened them again.

He carried on. He didn't understand it all, and yet everything was familiar to him. Every line of this children's edition wrenched tears from his eyes. What was happening?

Finally he had found the opening he'd been searching for when he was pounding the backs of the wardrobes. The window onto what he had left behind.

In almost three years, he had been unable to find a single link between the world into which he'd emerged and the labyrinth of his memories. There was a gulf separating them, and his attempts to traverse such an impassable precipice were feeding his madness. Should he believe what his memory was telling him? He was starting to think that his mind was full of nothing but illusions, a great void that he had populated with wild dreams about his love for a fairy.

But suddenly these pages before him, written in a language he barely understood, brought a familiar world rising to the surface. They weren't exactly about him or his past, but he recognized everything. The book spoke of the Kingdoms; of ill-fated princes and magic spells. All of it existed suddenly. His memory was there, printed on the paper.

He could feel tears rolling down the inside of his shirt collar.

His prison wall had just been breached. The crack was miniscule, almost invisible. But the rush of warm air billowed into the room and filled him with the hope, however mad, that somewhere there was a doorway, that someday he would return home.

He had to leave, to explore the world, to find the crossing.

He switched off the remaining lights and sat motionless for several hours in the glow cast by the streetlamp into *Maison Pearl.*

When the plasterer's three daughters came giggling and pressing their noses against the glass, he stashed the book away and went over to the door. They made signs at him and he let them in.

"You coming?"

Fresh from midnight mass, and still smelling of hot candle wax and incense, the girls were wrapped in their prettiest shawls, which hid everything but their eyes and the tops of their cheeks.

"What are you doing? Are you coming or what?" asked Suzanne, the eldest, who hardly ever spoke.

And off they set, their wooden heels dancing a foxtrot that rang down the street. He followed behind.

* * *

This was the first and last Christmas evening he ever spent with a real family: roasting chestnuts on the fire, three daughters huddled next to one another on a bench in the sitting room, a father moved to tears at welcoming this boy under his roof, a warmly lit room and a mistress of the house who, like so many others at that very moment across the city and the world over, apologised profusely about the taste of the chicken that was so scrumptious, so golden, so aromatic and so juicy beneath the crispy skin.

But even then, despite Suzanne's gaze and Colette's piercing laughter, the boy was on his feet between courses, heading to the window and parting the curtain slightly to look out on the street.

He knew already that he had to leave; that he would spend his whole life leaving.

Three days later, he was alone in the shop when the gendarmes turned up expecting to question Jacques Pearl again. The boy listened to them.

"He's not back yet."

"Perhaps you'll be able to give us the information we need."

There were three gendarmes. They explained that

there was absolutely no trace of Joshua Pearl's demise on the public record. They feared he was being concealed to avoid military service.

"With all that's going on, this is no time to shirk one's duty."

The boy looked around absent-mindedly.

"Do you understand?"

No. He didn't appear to understand.

"I need to speak to Joshua Pearl's father," said the gendarme.

He motioned to his colleague. This child was not behaving normally.

"What about you? Do have your papers?"

The boy took a long breath. He walked to the front of the counter, pulling off his apron.

"I am Joshua Pearl."

He had seized his chance to escape, like a tramp taking a running leap from an embankment onto the roof of a train without knowing its final destination.

He picked up his coat, scribbled a few words on a piece of paper by the till, and let himself be led off by the gendarmes.

Nine months later, in September 1939, war was declared.

He returned to Paris and went in uniform to kiss the

Pearls farewell. He was now a member of the French army's light cavalry, in the 2nd Spahi Regiment, on his way from Morocco to fight the Germans.

Jacques and Esther Pearl looked at the boy, framed by marshmallows and as handsome as any toy soldier. They didn't know that they were seeing him for the last time. Nor did they know that, sewn into each piece of his soldier's uniform, was the name he had stolen from them and that was now his own: the name of their dead son, Joshua Pearl.

9

ONCE UPON A TIME

As for where Pearl came from, the only thing I'm sure about are these first words, "Once upon a time".

The rest of what I write is based on what I've learnt since he appeared to me one autumn's day in front of his wall of suitcases. They amount to all I know of the world he was snatched away from.

*O*nce upon a time, there was a land ruled over by a king who was very much in love.

It often happened that the king, while travelling to his most far-flung provinces, would wake in the middle of the night and give orders to saddle his horse. Neither the fastest river nor the loftiest mountain would stop him. He changed horses at coaching inns on the roads winding through the forests. He would gallop for seven days and seven nights straight, just to be by his queen's side and watch her sleep.

The queen bore the king's first son. They named him Iån, after his father, his grandfather and all their other ancestors who had ruled the land for a thousand years. When Iån was seven years old, the queen fell pregnant again and, since that year it was unseasonably hot throughout the land, the king had a summer palace built for his wife in the middle of a lake surrounded by pine forests.

The building stood on stilts and was as light as the stroke of a quill. It could not have stood in greater contrast to the winter palace, which faced the sea and whose rough-edged towers traced dark, upward shapes that were lost in the clouds.

The queen lived at the small palace on the lake throughout her pregnancy. Currents of cool air drifted beneath the stilts. Prince Iån played on boats near by and caught trout with his hands. There, the king would spend what little freedom he was afforded by his vast realm and his people. In those days, he would rest his cheek against the queen's swollen belly and tell stories that thrilled the unborn child, making it quiver with pleasure. For in this land of fairy tales, stories from elsewhere set the rhythm of people's lives even before their first morning.

The three palace doctors came on a barge and informed the royal couple that they were expecting a little girl. Prince Iån, his pockets full of frogs, watched this assembly from his own boat. He scorned this child who was threatening to invade his land.

But there was always a famine, a civil war or a dragon to defeat at the other end of the world. There were glaciers positioned precariously above villages, ogres venturing out from their woods, and wolves. So it was that one day the king kissed his family farewell and left. His horse swam across the lake and took him far away. Before disappearing beyond the trees, he turned to look at the tiny palace made of reeds shimmering in the water. He saw from a distance the silhouette of Iån in his boat, glowering at his departure.

During those long weeks of absence, the queen became friendly with a young fairy who lived at the source of the lake, and who came to gather wicker from the banks by the summer palace. The queen adored this impetuous little fairy. Her name was Oliå. By her own hand she had woven the most beautiful white-wicker crib, which turned green in springtime.

The day of the birth was approaching. For months, the king hadn't returned from his voyage. In the beginning, the queen found solace in Oliå's visits. The fairy would arrive on the shore at nightfall and climb up the stilts with her bare feet, the bottom of her robe and her ankles dripping as though she had walked on water. But one evening, Oliå didn't come.

Prince Iån watched his mother pacing up and down the wooden pontoon, staring at the still lake until dark. In the end, Fåra, her old servant, brought her inside to sleep.

Twelve days later, Oliå still hadn't reappeared.

On the evening of the twelfth day, an unbearably hot night, a visitor was announced: it was Iån's godfather.

His name was Taåg. He was an old genie from the lowlands, three hundred leagues from the summer palace. Seven years earlier, he had saved the king as he was crossing the swamp on the way home to his wife. The royal steed had sunk in up to its flanks, and the king was at risk of being sucked under with it. This was around the time of Prince Iån's birth. The king had begged for help from Taåg, who lived nearby and heard his cries. The genie had caused the mud of the swamp to subside.

Once the horseman had escaped, Taåg released the foul water, and appeared flattered by the king's gratitude.

"Will Your Highness remember his servant?"

A few days later, the king invited him to become godfather to Iån, the child who had just been born.

The king soon regretted his choice. The queen feared Taåg's powers and kept him at a distance. But young Prince Iån worshipped his godfather.

And so it was that the seven-year-old prince was perched on his godfather's shoulders that twelfth evening when the genie of the marshlands visited the queen.

"Is the king here? I should like to speak with him," said Taåg.

A pool of sludge was spreading around his boots and across the floor, as Taåg leant on his staff, which was covered in fish scales.

"No, he's not here," answered the queen.

When Iån was aged three, Taåg had been denied permission to take the prince away with him to the marshlands where he wished to take charge of his education. The queen knew that he had never forgiven this affront.

Now, his dry eyes were trained on her. The queen did her utmost to appear undeterred. She was lying on a chaise-longue because of the heat, propping herself up on her elbows, hiding her belly behind a blue veil.

Her servant Fåra stood guard by her side.

"The king is not here," she repeated, forgetting that she had said this already. "Be gone with you."

Intrigued, Taåg could look at nothing but the round shape that swelled before his eyes.

"It would appear that he will be returning soon."

"I don't know," said the queen. "Leave me be."

Then, averting her gaze towards the lake, she noticed a grey line where the water had been shortly before.

"They say you're expecting a girl."

"I don't know," replied the queen, distracted.

Taåg was now looking at the same receding shore-line. The murky lake was descending in the darkness.

"Tell the king, if you see him, that I came to speak with him," he murmured.

"You're not staying?" asked the young prince.

His godfather rolled him gently across the floor, and by the time Iån had regained his balance on the muddy ground, Taåg had disappeared. The prince turned his eyes to the lake.

"Look," he said to his mother.

All across the lake, banks of mud were surfacing. Iån went out with a lantern in search of his little boat. The water level was so low that he found it hanging vertically from its mooring post, like a bat.

The following night there was not a breath of wind. The lake had dried up entirely, and a suffocating stench engulfed the palace. Clouds of mosquitoes rose up from the depths of the mire. Prince Iån was alone with his cries of joy early the next morning, when he was thrilled to discover little pools of water teeming with fish.

In the four corners of the summer palace, fires were laid with mud-drenched branches to chase away the mosquitoes. Smoke and ash came in through the doors and windows, clinging to the perspiring queen. After the second night, she was running a high fever. And when the alarm was sounded at dawn, the three family doctors found her too weak to be carried back to firm ground.

It was the hottest day of the summer. A procession of white fish bellies lay in the mud as far as the eye could see. At first, the young prince stayed at his mother's bedside, holding her hand. He had the bells rung to warn his father, and Fåra sent emissaries, but not one armoured horseman appeared at the bank between the pines. Through gritted teeth, Iån silently cursed the little princess, his sister, and he cursed his father for his absence.

Taåg sent an envoy to offer help. Iån begged the queen to accept: his godfather had mighty powers. But the queen drew on her last reserves of strength to dispatch the old genie's messenger.

It was a dreadful night. The queen's cries were lost in the lake. Iån blocked his ears and curled up below the palace, amongst the stilts.

Fåra kept watch over his queen, wringing out the linen cloths that he laid on her brow.

When the king returned the following day, he saw from afar the smoking braziers on the palace's pontoons. He crossed the lake on his horse to discover that the queen lay dead, surrounded by subjects wracked with grief. Iån was still by her side, along with Fåra. Nobody was minding the baby, who was sleeping peacefully, all brown with the bloody afterbirth, behind a paper screen. For the child had survived, and been cast into the crib without anyone paying it the least attention.

The three doctors laid their foreheads on the ground before the king, awaiting their punishment. But the king was no longer aware of anything. Prince Iån wouldn't even look him in the eye. To his mind, his father was just as guilty as the murderous infant.

The infatuated king went mad. Young Iån left for

the winter castle by the sea. He summoned Taåg, who made the water return to the lake. The king was shut away in the little summer palace with the newborn infant and the old servant Fåra. A fishing boat would occasionally drop off supplies. But soon a rumour spread that the palace's surroundings were haunted, and that any oarsman who went there would drown. Nobody ever returned.

The law of the Kingdoms dictated that Prince Iån had to wait until he was fifteen to be crowned. He took up residence in the towers of the castle, high up amongst the squawking gulls. At the tender age of seven, he made Taåg his advisor and regent while he awaited his coronation.

10

THE SOURCE OF THE LAKE

Thirteen years passed.

In the winter, the lake remained frozen and the stilts rose up above the snow. Only the edge of the forest traced the banks of the lake.

A man came out into the cold. He was wearing a fur cloak and thick mittens that made his hands look like the claws of a crab. It was Fåra, the queen's servant. His ageless face seemed carved from ice. He walked to the edge of the pontoon and turned to inspect the tiny empire over which he stood guard. In the summer, the holes in the walls and the mangled roofs let the air rush in, along with the rain and the birds. But all through the winter, the ruins of the palace were buried in snow, rendering it impenetrable.

Fåra retraced his steps, glancing left at the path in the snow, where the tracks were no larger than those of a white hare. He scanned the horizon keenly to try to see the much-loved little figure. But there wasn't a single movement anywhere. All was white and perfectly still.

Fåra returned to the palace.

"Where is she? Where is the sweet one?" a voice asked.

The king was sitting before the fire. He had heard Fåra enter.

"Is that you, Fåra?"

"Yes, Majesty."

"And the sweet one? Where is she hiding?"

"She died, Majesty. Thirteen years ago."

The king shook with silent laughter. When Fåra picked up the blankets that had fallen to his master's feet, the king grabbed him by the sleeve.

"Is she punishing me for my battles?" he whispered.

Fåra shook his head tenderly.

"She loved you, Majesty."

"Is it night?"

"No, it is day."

"So why does she insist on this endless sleeping?" asked the king, who knew of realms where the beauties woke up in the end.

"She died," Fåra repeated.

The king let out a sigh, a gentle sigh, as though weary of the queen's capricious games, as though her idleness kept her lingering in her bed.

"The sweet one."

Fåra had turned away to conceal his tears. Who cared for him in his grief? He had adored the queen, but each morning the king, in his madness, unwittingly reopened Fåra's wounds.

The old servant gladly thought instead about the white hare, who must have been running in the snow somewhere, and who was the palace's one consolation.

Several leagues from there, Iån had been ruling for five years. He was now twenty years old. His land was in a far more derelict state than the icy ruins resting on the lake. It was a land of tears. He had begun by plundering his people, emptying the forests of all their creatures, razing the cherry trees and wheat fields, and sowing fear everywhere. Out on the open sea, nets were cast down to the deepest waters where the last mermaids had found sanctuary. In the barns, unicorn meat was hung up to dry.

"Majesty, your archers have returned."

Taåg was standing at the young king's side. Though the years of his regency remained a bitter memory, Iån had succeeded in surpassing his former tutor's inhumanity.

"How many are they?"

"Eleven."

Following his godfather's lead, Iån had drained the land and was now eager to explore other realms, those whose stories were "done", and whose people were supposed to live happily ever after.

These people avoided venturing anywhere near the boundaries of lands whose stories were not yet done. But in the very first year of his reign, Iån had built a lightship on the reef to attract passing boats, only to then raid them.

No one could have imagined such a crime. Even Taåg had been locked in a tower for three years because he had reproached his master for attacking these realms. Having just been released after renouncing his criticism, he was now seeking to regain the king's favour.

The young king had decided to send fifteen of his finest mercenaries to prepare to invade.

"Only eleven archers have returned?"

"Yes, Majesty."

"Bring them to me."

Taåg covered his grey lips with the palm of his hand.

"First I must talk to you of a problem."

Despite recent years of both honour and humiliation, Taåg's face stayed true to its marshland origins, and he still left trails of mud in his wake.

"What problem?"

"The summer palace…"

Iån turned to Taåg. Not a soul had entered the palace since the death of the queen. The fishermen no longer even left food at the end of the pontoon.

"The old lunatic is dead?"

"I don't know."

"So?"

"There are tracks in the snow. Each day, someone is escaping from the summer palace."

"Who told you this?"

"The trapper who provides your skins."

Iån went over to the window as Taåg continued, "The king and his servant are too old to walk for hours in the snow. But there is perhaps…"

"Silence!"

Iån didn't need Taåg's prompting to recall the creature that had killed his mother during childbirth. The doctors had declared a daughter. Was she escaping to throttle the few remaining foxes and devour their flesh by sinking her black teeth into it? He pictured her as an evil beast made feral by her life in the wild. But could she have survived the solitude of the lake?

"Tell the trapper to watch her."

"No one has ever seen her…"

Iån turned abruptly to face his advisor, who stammered, "What should he do if he finds her?"

"Let him keep her skin to pay for the catch."

Taåg was not sure he had understood correctly.

"Majesty…"

"Don't pretend you didn't hear."

The white hare that kept escaping the decayed palace was not thirsting for the blood of foxes or lynxes. It fled the ruins before daybreak to cross the frozen lake without being seen by the lookouts.

It left silent marks in the snow. Not a sound, not even a whisper as it passed. A shadow amongst the shadows, fleet and stealthy.

And when the sun rose, it was already hidden away deep in the forest, where the light glided over it. Through the narrow slit of the creature's ermine cap, its eyes resembled those of the late queen. But this was no little princess – no, these eyes belong to a boy. A thirteen-year-old boy in a coat of white fur.

They had been expecting a girl, but a little boy had arrived instead, abandoned without a second glance in the crib. The old servant had named him Iliån, which means, "he who shall never reign".

He skirted round the lakeside without leaving the cover of the pines. Iliån was wearing the cord and leather pouch of a slingshot wrapped round his wrist. Each evening he would bring back the starlings he had shot from the topmost branches of the trees. But this morning, he didn't even look up when the wing of a bird disturbed the air. He was making for the source of the lake with a determined step.

The banks formed little coves that took an age to bypass. In summer he crossed them by swimming, but in wintertime, when the weather was clear, he didn't dare span the ice floe. He would have been too visible a target in this white landscape, so Iliån hugged the bank. It took him nearly three hours to reach the source of the lake.

The undergrowth became very thick. In springtime, it would be impassable. The source was in a sunken fold in the lakeside. This uneven corner was set amongst treacherous rocks and trees, all covered in snow.

A few days earlier, Iliån had crossed these barriers in the aftermath of a storm by digging through the snow, which had enveloped the whole area with a layer several feet thick. But already this snow was less even. In places, it had collapsed into crevices and the fine coating from the night before meant there were several hidden traps.

Finally he arrived at the snowy hollow above the source of the lake, which looked as smooth and soft as a feather cushion. There wasn't a single mark on the surface, but the stream could be heard trickling deep beneath the snow.

When he had discovered this place for the first time, after the blizzard, Iliån had spotted a ring of footprints on it. Bare feet that scarcely made any indent on the snow. These prints were unplaceable and didn't seem to lead anywhere, as if they traced the life cycle of someone born there one minute but who vanished the next. Thirty seconds in winter – a life more fleeting than a mayfly's.

But now there were no more footprints. The feather cushion was flawless.

Iliån lay down on a mound, at the foot of a tree, to scan the area. He had been raised by two old men, one of whom, his father, had lost all reason. All other living beings he kept at a safe distance of three hundred paces or more, even when he hid in the reeds or the branches to spy on them. These faint footprints had obsessed Iliån for days now. He knew the trapper's boot-marks and the deep grooves of his sledge, as well as the prints of all the animals round the lake, such as the four-toed egret in the summer mud, but these bare feet in the snow...

Flakes were beginning to fall. Iliån pricked up his ears. In the distance, he could hear howling.

Three hundred paces from there, the trapper was cracking his whip to silence his wolves. They were harnessed to a sledge, onto which he had trussed the body of a small white puma. The wounded beast had just fallen into a trap bristling with stakes on the other side of the lake. The puma was still breathing. Excited by this catch, the seven wolves now howled at a new scent they had just unearthed. The trapper brought them to a halt with cries and a few cracks of the whip. He dropped to his knees and looked down at the forest floor. The snow was falling more thickly now.

It was indeed her: the feral girl from the summer palace. He recognized the runaway's tracks. The powdery snow had barely been touched. His wolves huddled tightly around him, sniffing the bloody dagger strapped to their master's thigh.

Taåg had ordered him to catch her only if she escaped again. She had just passed through this place. Soon the tracks would be covered by the snow. He had to act fast. The wolves had fallen back in line, so the trapper climbed onto his sledge and followed the trail.

The pack rushed headlong between the trees. Once more the wolves had picked up the unmistakable scent of their quarry. They were entirely silent, their breathing muffled by the cottony snow. Ahead of them, the footprints were gradually becoming blotted out. Even the forest appeared to be dissolving before their eyes. In the freezing cold, the intense odours from the little puma suddenly began to throw the wolves' senses into confusion as they weaved and jostled between the trunks. The trapper tried to peer through the thick curtain of snow, the lash of his whip stinging the animals' backs.

Iliån didn't need eyes to find his way again. He continued forward through the vast whiteness. He thought of Fåra, who was awaiting his return at the palace. The wind was getting up. No doubt his father was sitting before the fire, regaling himself with tales of giants and a little girl in a red hood lost in the forest. These stories from other kingdoms represented the final frontier of sanity in his mind. Iliån had grown up in the presence of this man reduced to his memories, who held his hand aloft as he re-enacted the twirl of glass slippers around the ballroom.

Suddenly, two paces away from him, a noise stopped Iliån in his tracks. He caught his breath. The next instant, a seven-headed monster reared up out of the snow.

11

METAMORPHOSIS

The first wolf almost ripped its harness as it lurched forward to seize Iliån by the head. The leather straps stopped it in mid-flight as the boy rolled away in the snow to avoid the beast. Veering to one side, the rest of the pack thundered after him with a surge of energy.

At the back of the sledge, emerging from the cloud of powder, the trapper realized what had provoked the shock. In front of him, someone was plunging down the snowy valley. Finally he had found the little fugitive.

They were in a clearing on a slope. Now and then, the wind chased away the mist to reveal the trees down below. The sledge forged ahead without meeting any obstacles. Iliån skimmed over the snow as the hunter bellowed at his wolves.

"Kill!"

He had just drawn his dagger from his right thigh. He still hadn't seen the face of his prey, hidden as it was by the snow and wind. It was nothing but a silhouette that sliced through the air to keep ahead of the wolves. In a few seconds, she would be in the forest.

Once it had crossed the treeline, the sledge couldn't follow her through the tightly packed trunks. He only had a few dozen yards left to catch her.

The hunter leant forward and, with a slash of his dagger, cut the cords that held the body of the little puma. At the first hillock, the animal bounced off and slid down the piste, with its paws still tied. The sledge seemed to fly. Relieved of this load, the wolves felt as if the wind was propelling them forward. They were homing in on their prey.

Iliån was targeting the first trees, now so close, but he could feel the tornado of hot panting and animal smells behind him. This whirlwind was gaining on him.

Iliån knew the trapper. He'd seen him separating a litter of fox cubs from their mother with a pitchfork, and gutting game while it was still alive. He starved his wolves and pricked them to stir up their savagery. Above their cage, he hung sacks filled with blood.

The young prince heard the trapper howling at his pack, "Kill! Kill!"

The man would show him no pity. A ripple of fear drove Iliån a little further forward. The forest was there, just a few feet away.

"Kill!"

He reached the first pine just when the wolves were snapping at his heels. He thought he could feel the whip crack above his head, and his strength started to fail him. The snow was less thick beneath the trees, but Iliån was struggling to go any further. Behind him, claws tore at the ice and the sledge scraped the bark off the trees. Exhausted, and with his sight failing him, he lost balance and keeled over.

Right then, a commotion broke out. The harnessed wolves had just leapt between two twin pines, and the body of the sledge was now trapped in the fork. The seven beasts crashed into the snow, the breath knocked out of them. The trapper had been hurled against a tree and was groaning as he tried to stand up again, his right leg fractured.

Iliån was already on his feet; his face buried in the fur folds of his coat, ready to resume his flight.

The wolves were going mad, howling as they scrambled against each other, hobbled by their straps.

Iliån thought he was saved. But cruelty never sur-
renders easily.

The hunter had hitched himself up on his elbows
and was crawling, his dagger still in his hand. Iliån
watched him, unsure of what could justify such an
inordinate amount of effort: in his state, the trapper
would never make it as far as him.

Suddenly, the man gripped the wooden sledge,
yanked his arm to hoist up his powerless body, and
with a cry of pain he brought down his knife in a single
stroke, slicing the seven cords that held the wolves.

For a fraction of a second, time stood still.

Iliån leant against a trunk and gazed at the beasts,
who were stunned by their newfound freedom. The
very next instant, he saw them hurtling towards him,
jaws gaping and fangs glinting. His life was about to
end with this nightmarish vision when a gust of thick,
white wind stopped the pouncing wolves mid-flight,
covering them completely.

Iliån was waiting, fists clenched, for the moment
he'd be torn to pieces by the horde. Silence. Nothing.

And then, suddenly, their black shapes fell with a
heavy thud under the white veil. Strange grunts shook
the snow. A little further away, the cracked voice of the
trapper could be heard.

"Kill!"

There were the seven creatures, confused and disoriented, but their master didn't recognize them. They seemed to be bunched together, their bodies devoid of suppleness. The trapper saw great tufts of dark fur sprouting from the snow, rushing in circles, accompanied by anguished snorting.

One of the animals managed to break away from the frenzy, just a few feet from its wide-eyed master.

"The devil…"

Right there in front of him, a huge black wild boar had just reared its head. And then the others, one after the next, picked their snouts out of the snow, latching on to the hunter's scent.

He let out a cry of fear. What had become of the wolves from his sledge? The trapper looked around frantically: the fugitive had disappeared.

"The devil…" he muttered again, with his knife in his trembling hand.

As the slobbering boars started to bear down on him with their short legs, he saw the remains of the leather straps from the harnesses tethered to their backs.

Two hours later, Fåra scooped up Iliån's body from the snow near the summer palace.

He laid him out before the fireplace in front of the king, who eyed his son with an air of curiosity.

"You shelter passing pilgrims, Fåra... You bring honour to the palace."

"This is your son."

"Any lost child is my child."

"This is Iliån. He has lived with you for thirteen years. Ever since he was born."

The king listened attentively.

"Tell his mother to comfort him for a while."

"His mother is dead, Majesty."

A great sadness descended over the king's face. As he rose painstakingly from his chair, Fåra came to take his arm.

He helped him kneel down next to his son. The king seemed tired.

"Poor child," he said, "without his mother."

Fåra watched him stroking the boy's tousled hair.

"Poor child."

When the king stood up again, Fåra ushered him slowly across the room towards the alcove that served as his bedchamber.

"Once I had a little daughter who looked just like him," said the king as he lay down.

Fåra didn't have the strength to correct him.

"Good night, Majesty."

"Good night, Fåra."

Despite his illness, the king always recognized his old servant, just as a man instinctively finds his hand to protect himself or wipe away a tear.

Once the king had fallen asleep, Fåra turned towards Iliån, who was lying before the flames. The child had just opened his eyes.

"You stray too far from the palace, my prince."

Iliån smiled. What remained of palaces and princes in the Kingdoms? How had this servant succeeded in keeping the remnants of a forgotten world from tumbling down?

Single-handedly, Fåra was at once council, court, nurse and queen mother. He served also as the memory and the hands of the old king.

"I brought back some birds."

"Yes," said Fåra, "I will roast them this evening."

But Iliån was remembering his race through the snow, and the moment when he thought he had died.

"Who can turn a wolf into a wild boar?"

Fåra cast an anxious look at Iliån.

"Who is capable of that?"

The servant said nothing.

"Answer me, Fåra."

"Taåg is capable of that. Your brother's godfather."

"Who else?" insisted Iliån, who knew that Taåg would never have saved his life.

"In days gone by, certain magic-workers did that."

"Who?"

"Taåg has suppressed all the genies of the woods and streams. They are in hiding."

"Where are they?"

"I knew since the beginning that one day you would have to go away."

"Answer me. Where are they?"

"How am I to know? I never leave here. But if one of them did carry out that magic today…"

At that very instant, not far from there, Taåg knocked at a door with his scale-covered staff. The trapper was stretched out before him on a bearskin in his den, lit by the glow of a torch. His shattered leg was bound between two splints.

Snoring could be heard from the back of the cave.

"They're there," said the trapper, pointing to the metal grill behind him.

Taåg stepped into the shadows and put his hands on the bars.

The beady eyes of the boars penetrated the darkness.

"I had her," murmured the trapper. "She was just in front of me."

Through the bars, Taåg stirred the muck of the pigsty with his staff.

"They almost ate me alive," continued the invalid. "Find the girl who did this to me. Bring me back my wolves."

"Don't give me orders, you fool."

"And the puma? I had a white puma. It disappeared."

Taåg turned to him.

"It was almost dead in the snow," said the trapper. "Did it free itself from its shackles? Am I really to believe that?"

"Silence. Stop sniffling like your swine."

Taåg's face darkened.

"What was she like?" he asked.

"I never saw her face. She's small, but has the strength of a wild animal."

"Don't mock me. She is thirteen years old."

"I swear to you, it's true."

"It's not her. Someone was there and wanted to save her."

"Who?"

Taåg took the torch fixed to the wall and walked away.

"Don't leave me in the dark…"

Taåg left to join his men, who were waiting outside with their horses. One of them helped the old genie onto his steed. The trapper's moans could be heard from his cave.

Taåg shared the fire around the band's torches.

Two other genies lived hidden away on this side of the lake. Taåg had their forests burned. He was powerless against their magic, and could never annihilate them, but he wanted to make them quake with fear and weaken them further by destroying their land. If there were those who were committed to protecting the princess, then perhaps they meant to hand her Iån's crown. There had been talk of the first insurgents rising up amongst the people. The girl should have been eliminated long ago if she was a threat to their power.

All around him, Taåg saw flames leaping up in the forest as trees cracked and tumbled into the dark morass of charred wood and snow.

Iliån sat on the pontoon by the summer palace. He stared at the lake studded with animals fleeing the fire across the ice, and watched as the smoke rose up above the trees. Reindeer rushed by just next to him, and snow partridges sheltered beneath the palace stilts.

Iliån couldn't help thinking that he was the one who had lit the fire.

12

LOVE

It was the month of May. Cold rain was falling around her.

Standing up to her waist in the water, a girl was piling stones to strengthen the dam, in the place where the source of the lake sluiced over it. Each spring, the great thaw swept away the barrier, destroying the pool where she bathed.

With every new stone she added, the song of the little waterfall she created rang out more clearly. The level was rising around her as the water cascaded from higher up before disappearing into the irises of the stream below.

Oliå left the source each morning, cleansed of the previous day's experiences. The days and seasons never left a mark on her. She didn't age.

Even her mind was rejuvenated each morning, for

Oliå's youth was not limited to her appearance. Both inside and out, she had been fifteen years old for centuries. Not a day older.

Higher up, hidden in the rocks above the spring, Iliån was watching her. At last he had discovered whose tiny footprints had been haunting his every night since winter. They belonged to a fairy.

Crouching in the coolness of the shade, Iliån kept his gaze trained on her.

He had spent his life making himself invisible, maintaining the illusion of never being born. He knew how to melt into the scenery. Even the birds he hunted with his slingshot would fall without registering his existence.

Oliå seemed blissfully unconcerned about him or the rain.

She came out of the water and clambered across the pebbles. When she briefly disappeared from view, those seconds seemed like an eternity to Iliån. He felt them ticking away inside him as he craned his neck to keep her in sight.

When she reappeared at the edge of the pool, she was talking to someone behind her amongst the rocks. Turning towards the newcomer, who was outside

Iliån's field of vision, she squatted on her haunches, murmuring tenderly, holding out her hands and puckering her lips to entice him towards her. Who was she speaking to in this doe-eyed fashion? Iliån resented these fond gestures and smiles, this affection directed at a stranger. How he longed to hear her voice, lost beneath the rush of the water.

He crept forward slightly.

It was a small white puma, struggling to stand on his bandaged legs. He looked at Oliå devotedly, as if he had a great urge to go to her.

"Does it hurt?" she asked, her hands by her sides now, her voice deeper than her slight frame suggested. "Does it still hurt?"

Suddenly, the puma lifted his head, sniffed at the air and turned towards Iliån, who ducked too late.

He had been spotted.

He jumped onto the moss below, slid between two rocks and delved into the shadow of a thicket. Before he'd had a chance to take another step, she was already there.

The boy froze.

In front of him stood Oliå, her hair and dress still dripping. She was staring at the ground, more vexed than intimidated.

"If you get caught every time you go out, you'd be better off staying indoors."

Iliån hid his trembling hands in his sleeves.

"Was it you who helped me, back in the winter?" he asked.

"I don't know what you're talking about."

"The wolves…"

"What wolves?"

"You saved the little puma, too."

She looked up.

"At least he's learnt not to go running through the woods any more," she said.

"What's wrong with him?"

"The trapper slashed his hamstrings."

Iliån clenched his fists.

"The trapper doesn't kill outright," she added. "Meat keeps for longer when it's alive."

"He's a jackal, that man."

"Jackals don't harm anyone."

"Why did you protect me?"

At last she looked him in the eye.

The sky had cleared and they were left with the sweet smell that follows the rain.

"You mustn't go outdoors any more," she said. "They won't touch you so long as you remain in the palace. They would never be allowed to enter the resting place of a queen."

They looked at each other again, then she closed her eyes and suddenly seemed to become very distant.

Iliån felt as if he were being grabbed by the hand and dragged backwards through the green oaks. Yet Oliå hadn't moved; her fingers were still resting on the bark of the tree. As Iliån felt himself being whisked away, he was unable to put up any kind of resistance. He was being made to run over the brambles, his body and will impelled by an invisible force. He was eager to turn back to see her one last time, but the forest concealed them from each other.

An hour later, Iliån swam beneath the stilts of the palace and hauled himself up on a post to catch his breath. He felt the severing of the invisible thread that had caused him to flee.

Yet some forces are more powerful than magic. Another thread, a golden one, remained tied to the centre of his breast. A thread which he could never undo.

Iliån had grown up with his father's stories, told over endless nights and winters, but he had always sensed that there was a piece missing from the mechanism of these tales. Finally he understood the secret hiding behind all these stories, the mysterious cog that brought them springing to life; that turned ducks into swans, and caused jealousy and duels; that drove queens to despair, flung armies into battle or inspired the adventures of a valiant little tailor; that caused a king's madness.

With his feet in the water, still soaked in sweat from his running, he was beginning to discover the secret.

Despite Oliå's warnings, Iliån didn't remain secluded in his breezy palace. The very next day, he startled her near her pool. She chased him away, erecting walls of thorny bushes with a single stroke of her hand.

But the following day, he was back again.

And every day. Some nights, too.

Oliå's scolding became less convincing; none of her tricks kept him at bay for long. And when too much time elapsed between his forays, she would wander through the woods, sick with anxiety. Her memory spanned an eternity, but there was nothing in it to explain this numbness.

She stood at the ready, scanning the lake expectantly.

She too was discovering the same secret, forbidden to fairies: the life-affirming force of love, that brings with it birth and death.

PART TWO

KEEPING GRIEF ALIVE

13

Joshua Iliån Pearl

THERE WERE EIGHT OF THEM INSIDE, SOME SITTING, others lying against the cowshed walls. All the men were crouched under their horses, which dozed standing up. It was the 22 June 1941, and a series of battles had ripped through Lorraine in north-east France, close to the border with Germany.

They wore the uniform of the Moroccan Spahi Regiment and, with their capes and turbans covered in dust, they looked like desert cavalrymen lost in a war that didn't belong to them.

They had just taken refuge in this farm in the French countryside. Outside, the explosions had ceased. The silence was a foretaste of paradise.

"What about the flag?" came a voice.

The seven other men stiffened in the straw and stared at one another.

"Where's El Fassi?"

They were only there because they'd survived the bloodiest of battles, a month earlier and a little higher up the border in the Ardennes mountains. So they weren't about to leave one of theirs in some corner of a forest in Lorraine.

"Pearl?"

A young soldier had stood up.

"What are you doing, Pearl?" the lieutenant called out to him again.

"I'm off to find Corporal El Fassi, Lieutenant."

The troop had just fought for eight solid hours by a river, in an attempt to delay the advance of the German tanks. That was their mission in the face of the invader: to win time. In the end they'd had to retreat, collapsing behind these metre-thick walls to rally their remaining strength.

"I'll catch up with the rear," added Private Pearl.

"No, you're staying with us."

"But he has our flag, Lieutenant."

Catching the young soldier's eye in the gloom, the lieutenant appeared less assured now. They had mislaid their flag.

Of course, the missing corporal was far more than the group's standard-bearer. Brahim El Fassi was an heroic old soldier, whose beard made him look like an ancient prophet and who took care of everyone without a word ever passing his lips. In the deepest part of the desert, he let his horse drink from his flask first. But on the battlefield, men were no longer called El Fassi or Pearl, and the flag was worth at least fifty men. So it was because of the lost flag that the lieutenant changed his mind.

"Stop before nightfall if you haven't found anything. Don't play at being the hero."

While another Spahi opened the door wide for him, Joshua Pearl was already on his horse. He left behind a cloud of dust and hay in the cowshed.

It was eight o'clock in the evening, but Pearl instantly felt the heat hit him like the blast of a furnace. The burnt-out farm was still smoking and the earth was scorched from the sun that had beaten down on this second day of midsummer.

The first soldiers he encountered an hour later were also troopers. They were led by a young second lieutenant who galloped like a jockey, his knees tucked up by his shoulders.

"Are you lost?" he asked Pearl, slowing down to draw level with him.

"I'm looking for a corporal from the 2nd Spahis.

He should be carrying a pennant."

The Spahis didn't need a flag to be recognized. They always looked as if they had stepped out of a dance in *A Thousand and One Nights*.

"Stay with us," the officer advised Pearl, "it'll be dark soon."

Pearl thanked him, then swerved to the right and attacked the hill ahead of them. On reaching the summit, he realized that he was surrounded by woods, obscuring the overview he had hoped for. If he was to scan the valley before nightfall, he needed a higher vantage point. He jumped off his horse and made his way over to a tree. It was a beech with bark as smooth as leather, but he climbed the first branches in a matter of seconds. Meanwhile, his disorientated horse went round in circles, trying to find where its rider had disappeared to.

Pearl reached the top of the tree and poked his head out above the green mist of foliage. Squinting into the distance, he spotted green uniforms of a harsher hue manoeuvring at the foot of the hill. He recognized the German tanks.

This meant the enemy had breached all the barriers, and the corporal and his flag were likely to have been trampled along the way.

Pearl turned back towards the clearing. Somebody

was running in the direction of his tree. For a split-second, he thought it might be El Fassi, but further inspection revealed yet another fighter who had lost his way in the turmoil of war. The runner was German and weaponless. There was nothing orderly about the battles any more. Unlike those neat collections of toy soldiers lined up on shelves, these were battles that rose up from all sides; battles that dropped from the sky; battles that burst out of the earth or hurtled down slopes with no warning.

Pearl began his descent in the half-light, feeling for the branches with his feet. Once back in the main part of the tree, he heard a whinnying sound. He glanced down, guessing that the soldier had jumped onto his horse and was digging his heels into its flanks. The rider let out a cry as Pearl was poised to jump down. But it was too late: the horse had already bolted, the sound of its galloping hooves fading into the distance.

After a safe landing, Pearl leant against the tree trunk and took stock. Without his horse, his best chance lay in darkness falling swiftly. But minutes later, the freshly-mounted soldier reappeared in the clearing, and this time he wasn't alone: two German motorbikes were bouncing along behind him. The thief had called in reinforcements.

Pearl began to run across the field without holding out much hope. The throbbing of the motorbikes was getting closer, and the sound of gunfire rang out. Just then, through the hail of bullets that made the earth fly up around him, he glimpsed a horseman emerging from the depths of the forest, like some divine vision. The trooper brandished the flag of the 2nd Moroccan Spahi Regiment, his cape shone white in the evening light, and his turban was immaculate.

Corporal El Fassi set his horse in the opposite direction, galloping in a great loop around the clearing before he made for Pearl in earnest, whisking him up onto the saddle behind him. The motorbikes were right behind them now and the explosions intensified, but Pearl clung to his companion. The horse jumped over two fallen trees and they entered the forest.

Their ride felt glorious at first. As they snaked their way between the trees they sensed that their pursuers had given up the fight, and the din was fading behind them. Darkness was descending. With his arms around his fellow trooper, Pearl felt safe in the intoxicating cool that reminded him of the forests of his childhood.

The horse beneath him was still going strong, but Private Pearl suddenly had concerns about the rider.

Although the flag flew high, the man holding it seemed to have slumped.

"Corporal?"

His only answer was a faint sigh, as the body began to lurch to the side. Pearl held onto him with all his might, grabbing the reins and making the horse slow down.

"Are you wounded, Corporal El Fassi?"

"Perhaps."

Just as they were leaving the forest, the moonlight exposed a huge bloodstain on the standard-bearer's white cape, and the red was spreading. A bullet had struck him in the chest, as he was carrying out the rescue.

Pearl's arms grappled to keep his fellow trooper on his mount. The corporal's body had gone limp, with the exception of his hand, which clung desperately to the shaft of the flagpole.

"Leave me here," said El Fassi.

Pearl knew they couldn't advance much further, and he steered the horse towards a stream he could hear lower down. For a few minutes they followed the shimmering watercourse beneath the moon, and the sound of hooves rang out over the pebbles.

They came to a stop under a great stone bridge, which must have had a road or a railway passing over it. Pearl laid the wounded man down by the water's edge, in the shelter of the arch. He ripped through El Fassi's clothing with his combat knife, freeing his shoulder and chest. When he lifted up the corporal, he saw that the bullet had gone straight through him, and he could feel the wound on both sides. El Fassi continued to breathe without complaining. The bullet had passed so close to his heart that Pearl thought it was all over.

"I just have to make it through the night," said El Fassi, who wasn't used to speaking at such length. "If I can make it through the night, I'll rally again."

It was the trembling of the horse's hooves in the water that they heard first. Then came the thunderclap. The corporal smiled when he understood this was not the sound of war.

The rain started to fall on either side of their shelter, as Pearl fashioned a bandage from the strips of torn shirt. The bullet had made a clean exit: there was nothing left to do but wait.

Pearl put his cape over the horseman and lay down next to him. They listened to heavy summer rain, cascading like a waterfall, while flashes of lightning illuminated their shelter. With each thunderclap, Joshua Pearl recalled the night when he had passed from one world to another. Was his companion about to make a journey in the opposite direction?

After an hour, Private Pearl noticed the wounded man's breathing becoming more rasping. He stood up, wetted the flag in the stream, and placed it on his eyes and forehead.

"Say something," whispered the standard-bearer.

Fate had conspired to bring together the two least talkative soldiers in all of France and her empire. Pearl didn't know what to say, but when El Fassi let out a groan the young soldier knew it was his duty to break the silence. Pearl owed the corporal his life. Now it was his turn to soften his death.

"Tell me something."

And so Pearl searched deep inside him for what was most precious.

"I was born far from here," he began.

"Me too," gasped the corporal, who was remembering a small village in the sands, thousands of kilometres from there.

It was midnight. Joshua Iliân Pearl spoke until dawn, and he confessed everything: even that which he had sworn never to reveal.

At dawn, the corporal was still alive.

* * *

On the morning of the 23 June 1941, a German armoured division picked up two stray soldiers and a lone horse close to Sion hill in the Lorraine region. One of the men was treated in a makeshift infirmary, under the watchful eye of the second, before they were both sent across the border to a prison camp in Westphalia, Germany.

In France, the fighting was over. The war was lost, and the country occupied.

14

THE MERMAID'S SCALE

The letter began with *Our Joshua*. The prisoner who
had opened it, standing against the hut with his feet
in the snow, found this very moving. Jacques Pearl
must also have felt emotional as he wrote those words,
sitting in the small Parisian dining room, his wife by
his side. With the pencil between his fingers, he would
have felt the heat of the oven, and inhaled the aroma of
chestnut flour in the bread.

Our Joshua,

*We received your letter two weeks ago. We haven't
slept much in all this time. When the envelope arrived,
with that name written on the back, I thought it was
my turn to die. I waited until evening to open it.
Today, we're replying because it's Christmas. As you
know, the shop is closed. We're both in our dressing*

gowns. It feels strange. It's almost midnight.

I wrote "our Joshua", because that's what you're asking of me, on account of the guards reading the prisoners' letters. (Evening, gentlemen!) But now I'm writing it again just for the pleasure of it, because it's so sweet to see it on paper. Dear Joshua, our little one, don't think that your letter hurt us. Don't think that.

The prisoner's eyes welled up. He had written to the Pearls just before the winter, prompted by a man he had worked with for ten days when they were assigned to clean the camp water reservoir. They were the only two French-speaking soldiers on shift. The other man had been so delighted to rediscover his language that he had recounted his life story during their time together in the mud. He explained that his parents had asked him to stay in captivity for as long as possible. His family ran a hotel in the north of France. They were Jewish and they'd had problems with the police before, but now they were left in peace on account of their son being a prisoner of war in Germany.

While he was rotting in this camp, eaten alive by fleas, his parents' plush establishment, with the piano in the hall and the view over the river from the breakfast room, could remain open. The man said it suited him; that his only fear was dying of typhus before the war was over.

"If I die, the hotel will be shut down."

Hearing that story had made Joshua think of *Maison Pearl*. He'd never written, not once since the outbreak of war, so as to avoid writing his name in any correspondence and revealing to Jacques and Esther Pearl that he had slipped into the uniform of their dead son. But suddenly he'd understood how he might be able to help them in turn: by letting it be known that one Joshua Pearl, a worthy soldier, had been a prisoner for nearly two years as a result of fighting for France.

Yes, Jacques Pearl's letter went on, *the authorities aren't making our life easy at the moment, but I have faith in my old country. They won't find it so easy to get rid of us!*

So, for now, I don't wish to take your advice by mentioning your name to the police. It wouldn't feel right, telling them I had a son in captivity. And anyway, the shop is still open for business. There are people who are much worse off than we are. I'm enclosing a photo of the shop window last week, before Christmas, so that you don't worry about us. The pharmacist took the photo for you. Doesn't it look smart?

And there it was… He hadn't noticed it before, but at the bottom of the envelope Joshua found a photo of *Maison Pearl* all lit up in the snow, with another reassuring message in the corner:

> *Christmas soon. As you can see!*
> *Business is good.*
> *The shop's doing well, etc.*

In the letter, Jacques Pearl showed his concern for the hardship faced by the prisoner: he said he planned to put together a parcel with warm clothes and marsh-mallows for Joshua and his army pals. He listed the few flavours of marshmallow they were still able to produce, despite the rationing. He spoke of the sacks of walnuts he had miraculously found one autumn morning, in the back room of the shop, and which had saved the season. And then there were the almonds from the Pilon farm, which had never been so good.

Finally, he wrote about a female shop assistant who had appeared in September and who had proved inval-uable to them following the young man's departure.

She works so well, and is so kind that of course Madame Pearl wants to introduce her to you on your return.

I had asked her to be in the photo, so that you could see her. She was sitting on the boxes, but she must have slipped out of the frame just as the pharmacist was pressing the shutter, you know what girls are like. She enjoys it when I tell her about you. Oh, and did I mention that she's very beautiful?

On closer inspection, Joshua could indeed see small footsteps in the snow around the boxes.

At the end of the letter, there were a few lines in which Jacques Pearl, deliberately writing in caged terms to put the guards off the scent, expressed his impatience to see him back, to speak with him and to understand why he had left like that, taking the name of a dead child.

Joshua folded the letter. Despite the cold burning his fingers, he had a warm feeling inside. He slid the envelope into his pocket, no longer burdened with being an imposter.

It was the beginning of February 1942, and he had just survived a succession of interminable seasons as a German prisoner of war in this stalag. He worked outside, mainly in the forest, where groups of prisoners were marshalled to transport tree trunks. Most of the prisoners in the camp were Polish. They were starving, fed only on soup as clear as rainwater. The French were a little better treated by the German guards, but disease, sickness, fleas and violence made life difficult.

Joshua Pearl returned to his dormitory, where the bunks were stacked three-high along the walls. He sat down at the back, on the edge of the bottom bunk.

"I've received a letter," he told a shadow lying on the other side of the narrow aisle between the bunks.

Brahim El Fassi rolled over to face him. A strong bond had formed between these two men since their night below the bridge in the storm. Joshua had confided everything, in the belief that the horseman would take that precious knowledge to his death. Some stories ease the moment of departure. But this story had worked like a magic potion. *If I can make it through the night, I'll rally again*, El Fassi had vowed. It was the voice of Iliån that had helped him to make it through the night. He had rallied.

For several days, in a school in Nancy that had been transformed by the Germans into a temporary prison and hospital, the two soldiers were barely able to exchange glances. It was as if they were embarrassed at having survived that long night.

Now, they had become inseparable. But they had never mentioned Iliån's revelations again.

"Is it a good letter?" asked El Fassi.

"Yes. It's a good letter."

A slight twitch of his beard betrayed the corporal's satisfaction.

A good letter. That was all he needed to know. He sat up, unrolling the coat that served as his pillow, and put it on. Non-matching items of uniform, ripped from the battlefield, were doled out to the prisoners. El Fassi had, however, been allowed to keep his Spahi turban.

Standing up, he signalled to Pearl to follow him. They stepped over the prisoners on the floor playing cards in woollen gloves. Brahim El Fassi pushed open the door and went outside into the snow.

When they were far enough away from the huts, El Fassi began to speak, uttering each sentence as if it were the result of long consideration.

"I went to the infirmary for my wound, Private Pearl."

They were always courteous and respectful, generally addressing one another by their regimental title, after all these months of sharing the same hardships. Perhaps it was a way of preserving the remnants of civilisation beneath the rubble.

"Are you in pain?"

"Not much."

Pearl knew that he was lying. The corporal suffered every night, and slept with his belt between his teeth so that no one would hear him grinding them in agony.

"But the doctor speaks French," said El Fassi. "He's from Alsace, and he knows my country as well. He tells me things. I appreciate that."

By some miracle, Pearl hadn't yet needed to visit the camp infirmary. He found it hard to believe that anyone would go there of their own free will. But the corporal was talking as never before.

"He pointed out a Polish man who comes to see him every morning for his lungs."

Silence, and then, "He's a prisoner, but he works for the camp guards. He polices his whole block. Even the doctor is scared of him."

Pearl was straining his ears to catch El Fassi's hushed tones.

"His name is Bartosz Kozowski, but everyone calls him Kozo."

They walked the length of the barbed wire fence in silence, crossing paths with ten men who were laden with stakes and sacks of cement.

"If you need me..." Pearl ventured, when they'd overtaken them.

"No."

"Then why are you telling me about this Polish man?"

"I shouldn't be. He fills the camp cemetery with anyone who gets in his way."

El Fassi glanced around to see whether the groups of prisoners were far enough off now. Next, he checked the watchtower before saying, in an even quieter whisper, "Kozo wears something around his neck. The doctor told me about it. And—"

"And?"

"It's a mermaid's scale."

Pearl froze.

"It's attached to a silver cord. He showed it to the doctor, who says he's never seen anything like it."

They had reached the end of the barbed wire fence, and found themselves opposite a brick hangar.

El Fassi stared straight into his friend's eyes.

For the second time in his life as an exile, Pearl felt the breath of air at his back which linked him to his former world. The first time had been on discovering the book of fairy tales that last Christmas Eve at *Maison Pearl*.

Further off, a short man in an oversized coat came out of the hangar, coughing in the snow. Brahim El Fassi watched Pearl and saw in his eye a grey glint that flashed like a mermaid's scale.

153

The man who had just emerged kept coughing, bent over double, flanked by two armed guards. As Pearl watched them approaching, he wondered where they were taking the patient.

In the nightmare of the prison camp, he had always imagined escaping. It had become an obsession. But now he knew that he couldn't leave without uncovering the mystery revealed to him by his friend. The only true escape was the one that would lead him back to where he belonged. If Kozowski's scale really did exist, then it must have traced a path between this world and the story world. The mermaid's scale would surely lead him back to the Kingdoms.

"Where's the doctor?" asked Pearl.

"Inside that hangar."

"What about Kozo?"

"Just behind you."

The sickly man and his two guards passed by very close to them. He spat in the snow.

Pearl just had time to glimpse his face.

15

LIKE A LITTLE SNAKE

The next day, Joshua Pearl was taken to the infirmary. He looked all done in, half his face covered by a bloody bruise. El Fassi had eventually given in and punched his friend in the face.

He certainly hadn't missed his target.

Situated at the end of the camp, the inside of the hangar looked like a place where people went to die, even though the most serious cases, those patients suffering from tuberculosis or typhus, had been isolated in other buildings.

Pearl was pushed to one side and made to wait in line for the only doctor who spoke French.

He waited for some time, assaulted by the smell of ether and the complaints of the sick. German guards moved between the rows of beds.

Finally, the doctor appeared.

"A fight?"

"Yes."

He examined the eye by lifting the eyelid with his thumb.

"Who did this?"

Pearl remained silent.

"You can tell me, I won't repeat it to anybody. I'm a prisoner myself. Who hit you?"

"A soldier called El Fassi."

The doctor wrinkled his nose.

"I know him. He doesn't hit."

"Unless a friend asked him politely."

This time, the doctor took his hands away from Joshua Pearl's face.

"I have come to speak with you about Bartosz Kozowski," his patient went on.

The doctor glanced around at the sick and ailing prisoners on their mattresses: most of them looked asleep.

"If it's the cornea, I need to take a proper look in the daylight."

Pearl followed the doctor towards the door.

"He's more powerful than me," the doctor muttered under his breath as he walked.

"I know."

"He often dines with the camp commander. He

paid a high price for his power."

"Using what?"

A German soldier passed by close to them.

"Sorry?"

"What did he pay with?"

"Kozo intercepts the French parcels," replied the doctor with a shrug.

Only the French were allowed to receive parcels, because of an agreement between the governments of the two countries.

"Tins of sardines won't buy you the commander of this camp."

The doctor stared hard at Pearl.

"Well, did your friend El Fassi tell you?"

"Yes."

Only Joshua Pearl's direct gaze and honest voice could explain the trust of a man who'd met him for the first time moments earlier.

"What if the scale is a fake?" asked Pearl, now that they were outside the hangar.

"I saw it, around his neck…"

The doctor lowered his eyes and seemed to grow more distant.

"I've travelled a great deal," he went on. "I've followed archaeologists, looking after them in Egypt and elsewhere. I've seen real treasure. But this time, I know that it's not from this world."

The doctor still seemed to be haunted by his sighting of the scale.

"Does he frighten you?" asked Pearl.

"I see what happens to those he didn't appreciate, when they pass through here, and it's a good reason to be frightened."

The doctor was in two minds about whether to carry on.

"There's something more serious."

This time, he turned around to check that nobody was hiding in the mud-streaked snow.

"Kozo is sick," he whispered. "I'm the only person who knows. He doesn't want to be locked up in Block T, the building for tuberculosis sufferers: he's contaminating the whole camp."

"I can get rid of him for you, with your help."

The doctor went back inside the hangar, and Pearl followed as they passed close to the sickbeds.

"Well?" asked Pearl, when the doctor stopped at a basin to wash his hands.

"There doesn't appear to be any serious damage to the eye, but I'll bandage it up for you just in case. Come back to see me tomorrow. You can never be too careful."

* * *

Pearl returned the following day, having already obtained permission to change dormitory and barracks. After the fight with prisoner El Fassi, he didn't want any further contact with him. The staging of this separation was very painful for the two friends, but it was key to their plan. Kozo mustn't suspect any collusion between them.

Three days later, during their secret early morning consultation, the doctor informed the fearsome Bartosz Kozowski that a prisoner had found out about his illness and was threatening to reveal it.

The squat man turned deathly pale.

"And you let him get away?" he demanded, grabbing the doctor's throat.

"A second prisoner is also in the know. He claims he'll tell all, if anything happens to the first one."

Never before had Kozo been victim to this kind of blackmail. He didn't give anyone the chance to dictate the terms. It was simpler that way. With both thumbs, he increased the pressure on the doctor's windpipe.

"Are you his messenger?"

"I could have chosen to keep quiet and not mention it to you."

"Except that if I fall, you fall with me."

"Another reason to be on your side," said the doctor. "In keeping your secret, I may have allowed men to become contaminated. I'm as guilty as you are."

Kozo let him fall back into his chair.

"I'm not guilty of anything," he declared, wiping his hands on his coat.

They were in a tiny office with a window at the top of a staircase, looking out over all the rows of stretchers. Kozo coughed and leant against the glass with his shoulder: the little cogs of his minuscule brain were clicking back into action.

"What are they asking for?"

"An escape plan…"

"The swines!"

"One other thing…"

"What?"

"They want that."

The doctor was pointing at the middle of Kozo's chest.

"Me?"

"No, the scale. And they want to know where it comes from."

Bartosz Kozowski began to cough very loudly indeed, leaning with both hands against the wall.

He then made several attempts to ask a question that clung stubbornly to the bottom of his lungs, before emerging as a whimper.

"Who is it?"

"He's called El Fassi. Brahim El Fassi."

In the days that followed, Pearl noticed that El Fassi was being tailed closely by a small group of Polish prisoners who watched his every movement.

They must have been rather disappointed by their subject. El Fassi had been requisitioned to repair a roof that had caved in under the weight of the snow, he didn't say a word to anyone and he never stopped working. The men shadowing him were tasked with discovering the identity of his accomplice. But for now, El Fassi's only accomplices were his hammer and his bag of nails.

Joshua Pearl watched at a distance, touched by what his friend had agreed to do for him. They had long since developed an unconditional solidarity. They no longer kept a tally of who had last taken a risk for the other. They simply did what they felt needed doing.

At nine o'clock in the evening, just as Pearl was due to return to his dormitory, he ran into El Fassi being dragged off by two men. They didn't dare exchange glances. From curfew and throughout the rest of the night, Pearl was convinced he could hear cries from the other end of the camp.

At dawn, however, El Fassi was back at work on the roof with his tools and pine planks.

This time, as Pearl passed down on the path below, he dared to smile at the regular beat of the hammer. No response. This troubled Joshua. Then he spotted a young man in a hat, posted a few metres away, who never took his eyes off El Fassi. He understood that they mustn't put a foot wrong. A smile could prove fatal. The pact uniting them had to remain invisible.

Visiting the infirmary for the last time, to get the dressing replaced on the wound that had long since healed, Pearl found out what had happened during the night. The doctor had been present throughout.

El Fassi had arrived at nightfall, led by two burly Polish men. Kozo was waiting behind the hangar, near a mound of coal. He had asked his men to step aside. The doctor had remained close by.

Kozo had pointed out the mound of coal to El Fassi.

"If I bury you in there, nobody'll find you before the spring."

He spoke perfect French.

"Indeed," El Fassi answered calmly.

Kozo walked right up to El Fassi, who thrust his hands deeper into his coat pockets before continuing.

"But if you bury me in there, you'll be buried just a bit further off, and well before the spring…"

The confidence with which he expressed every word had the effect of making his desert accent disappear.

"Tuberculosis sufferers don't survive two weeks when they're locked up in Block T."

Kozo froze.

"Who says you really have an accomplice?" he asked eventually.

"I do."

"And if you're lying?"

"That's a risk you'll have to take," El Fassi shrugged. "You can always kill me, then wait to see what happens."

Kozo felt the net tightening around his body. Sometimes the simplest traps are the most deadly. He couldn't touch a hair beneath this man's turban without another prisoner spreading the rumour somewhere else in the camp. The link between Brahim El Fassi and the unknown prisoner made them invincible.

"You're lying," said Kozo. "I can tell you're lying."

El Fassi didn't respond. The doctor followed the scene with a mixture of terror and gratitude. For as long as he'd been the only person who knew, he was powerless against Kozowski. But the two friends might finally rid the camp of this bully.

"And the scale?" asked Kozo.

"I want to know where it comes from."

All that was visible was the silver cord inside the coat collar, below Kozowski's ear.

"Well?" Pearl asked the doctor, who was relaying the previous night's encounter while removing the young soldier's dressing.

"Nothing. He hasn't revealed anything yet."

When he leant over the boy's face, the doctor noticed how pale he looked. Why was he so interested in this mermaid's scale?

"If I were you, I wouldn't worry about such things," he advised Pearl. "In the pyramids of Egypt, I witnessed men losing their minds in the quest to grasp such mysteries. Be very careful. If something has come from another world, then it may also have deadly powers."

Joshua Iliån Pearl didn't respond. How could he talk to this man about his kingdom, and about the love that perhaps awaited him there? Iliån had been abandoned in the great woods of our planet. And any tiny pebbles or scales that came from the Kingdoms might represent his only way of return.

That same evening, at midnight, the prisoners were

woken by the sound of boots kicking at the hut doors. Pearl sat up in bed. It was cold, but the men around him were starting to get dressed. One of the German guards barked out a list of prisoners.

A one hundred year-old oak had fallen on the railway line a few kilometres from the camp, bringing down ten trees with it. The train carrying passengers from Berlin was stuck on the rails. The prisoners were ordered to leave at the double in order to free the railway line.

On hearing his number being called out, Pearl got up and groped for his shoes in the dark. A few prisoners fell in alongside him. He was astonished that the summons only applied to half his dormitory. Usually there was no selection process: conscription was by whole huts at a time.

Outside, he saw other soldiers filing out of different buildings in the glare of the tower's searchlights. The prisoners were drawn up four by four. There must have been about thirty of them, guarded by twelve soldiers and their dogs. Saws and axes had already been loaded into two lorries, as the prisoners clambered onto the wooden benches at the back.

In the midst of all this commotion, Pearl spotted El Fassi climbing into the other lorry. This time their eyes met, and the soldier saw the corporal putting his hand on his heart to show him something. As he did so, a torch swept across El Fassi's face and Pearl saw something glinting around his friend's neck like a little snake: it was the silver cord. Then El Fassi disappeared beneath the lorry's tarpaulin.

16

THE TRAIN

As they trooped alongside the train to reach the fallen trees, the prisoners couldn't help peering inside the halted carriages, like children gazing at a life-sized Christmas nativity scene.

It was all lit up inside. Ladies with immaculate hairdos were wrapped tightly in blankets. Steaming drinks were being passed from hand-to-hand. The men were reading newspapers, while small children could be glimpsed sleeping in the luggage racks above the windows. A few older gentlemen were smoking by the doors as they watched the shadows of the convicts filing past.

As far as all the passengers were concerned, this incident represented the height of discomfort and adventure. Would they reach their friends in Dortmund on time? Would they have to ration their cigars until they reached the next station? Above all, how could they keep the children from being frightened? They could hardly have imagined that, at the same time, the prisoners outside their windows were dreaming of a crust of bread in tomorrow's soup, or working out the best way to squash a flea between two frozen fingers.

Two worlds were rubbing shoulders in the night.

But Joshua Pearl hadn't even glanced at the carriages. His eyes were firmly on El Fassi's turban, twenty metres ahead. He had to speak with him. The men immediately in front were walking in single file, since straying from the stones of the railway track meant sinking into the mud.

They had all heard the word "sabotage" being repeated in German by two passengers at a window. When they arrived at the trees blocking the way, the rumour was confirmed.

The great oak had been chopped cleanly at its base. This could only be an act of terrorism. Luckily, the train had slowed down for a level crossing, grinding to a halt in time.

The axes could already be heard thudding into the trunks. Spotting that El Fassi had picked up a saw, Pearl stepped over a branch to join him, but the corporal rushed towards another prisoner who was standing idly by. Pearl understood the warning: they mustn't be seen together.

Dogs could be heard barking a little way off, beyond the noise of sawdust and wood-shavings being produced. Meanwhile, the guards had formed a ring around the thirty prisoners, caught in the beam of the engine headlights.

Pearl had chosen an axe, and they made swift progress as sections of trunk were rolled into the ditch.

Suddenly, El Fassi was next to him, tugging at the same branch that formed a screen of pine needles.

"To the right, look."

Pearl turned his head.

"The guard with two dogs has been tipped off: he'll let us through. There's a hut five hundred metres from here with clothes and a map."

"We shouldn't trust Kozo," Pearl hissed through gritted teeth. "Let's head in the opposite direction."

"He wouldn't lie. He has nothing to gain from us getting caught; otherwise he's a dead man."

The branch they were dragging got stuck in the brambles.

"Why trust him?"

"I have the scale."

"Where did he find it?"

"I'll tell you everything."

They were approaching a heap of boughs by the edge of the ditch, and beyond the beams of light. A guard was positioned there with two dogs that panted as they strained on their leashes.

"Follow me."

They took a few more steps and lifted up the pine branch. Before it hit the ground, El Fassi had dived into the undergrowth with Pearl quick on his tail. The dogs growled, held in check by the soldier who was looking the other way.

The two fugitives crawled through the foliage and pine needles. They could hear the axe-blows and the shouts behind them, mingled with the steamy breath of the train. El Fassi was the first to emerge on the other side. Seeing that the path was clear, he held out his hand to Pearl, who pulled himself up next to his friend. The first trees beckoned, only two steps away.

The fugitives were running side by side in the dark now. Pearl was thinking about the secrets that Kozo had revealed to El Fassi. Where had the scale come from? Was there an opening back to the Kingdoms? His answer was just at his shoulder, darting between the tree trunks.

"Who made the trees fall on the line?" asked Pearl.

"He did. He set everything up."

A feeble light glimmered ahead of them in the woods. Pearl slowed down.

"Is someone expecting us?"

"He organized for a lamp to be put in the house."

Pearl's instincts were telling him to head in a different direction. To get away from there. The scale, the secret and their freedom: it was all too much at once. They couldn't trust in anybody or anything now, not even luck.

"Wait," he whispered to his friend.

They stopped, gasping for breath under the pines. The hut was in the middle of a tiny clearing, twenty or thirty metres off.

"We should make do with what we've got," insisted Joshua.

"It's all going to plan, just the way he said it would. He hasn't lied to us so far."

"So far, yes, but…"

"He wants to protect himself. It's in his interest to keep us at a distance."

Even as he was speaking, El Fassi recalled the hatred that had smouldered in Kozo's eyes; but he also knew they were hundreds of kilometres from the

French border and that neither of them spoke German. What could they do without a map or a compass, and in these clothes?

"We can manage," said Pearl. Over there, the faint light was glowing in the window of the hut.

"Look at me," said Brahim El Fassi very seriously. "Look at me carefully."

Despite the inky blackness, Pearl could make out his friend's deeply lined face and those eyes as dark as his skin. How was he supposed to cross Germany in 1942, with features like his?

"So? Do you still believe we can?"

"I know all about forests," said Joshua Pearl. "I know how to keep hidden, cross rivers and find invisible paths. I'll lead the way. I promise you we'll make it."

He pointed in another direction while, in the distance, the whistle sounded from the train departing. But El Fassi was no longer there. He had rushed into the clearing. Just as Pearl made to follow him, a burst of machine-gun fire blew out the hut windows, and swept across the undergrowth.

Pearl saw his friend being flung into the air and come crumpling back down again. The flames from the machine gun blasted through the window as the bullets hailed down. Pearl was fixed to the spot. He saw the gun switch aim and begin to fire at him with the same intensity, making the bark on the tree erupt and throwing up the earth and frost-covered leaves at his feet.

He cast a final look at Brahim El Fassi's lifeless body in the long grass. It was all over. He understood there was nothing for it but to flee.

There were soldiers rushing out of the hut, and more with dogs closing in on him from behind. But once again Pearl had the reflexes of a hunted animal. As he leapt between the trees he knew exactly what he had to do, despite the sweat blurring his vision.

Yes, if El Fassi had listened, Joshua would have helped him return home. He had escaped from other chases, from other impossible crossings. He would have led his friend back to the heart of his desert, back to his village in the sands.

Reinforcements were arriving from the stalag. The woods were staked out, and there were temporary roadblocks at every crossroads for a radius of ten kilometres. Kozo's men even forced the villagers to comb the area with their hunting guns. But the fugitive was nowhere to be found.

* * *

A hundred kilometres away, the train was slicing through the fog. The driver had made up for some of the two-hour delay by charging full speed ahead through the freezing night. Dawn was breaking, and most of the passengers were asleep. Joshua Pearl kept an eye on them, sitting by the window in a velvet suit that was much too big for him, and which he had removed from a suitcase in the first class carriage.

His hand had been injured while hoisting himself up onto the moving train. Now, his fist was clenched inside his sleeve and his head hung low. He watched the water droplets rolling horizontally across the window, level with his eyes. The whiff of wax from the carriage seat, mingled with a female traveller's eau de Cologne, reminded him of Madame Pearl's dining room in Paris. A little girl was staring soberly at him from the arms of her dozing mother.

He had just lost his only friend and destroyed the delicate trail that might have led him back to his realm and to the buried layers of his memory. But he also had to acknowledge that he was now forming memories on this earth.

These were his first tastes of nostalgia since arriving here.

It was because of the tenderness of certain moments

in our world that he would have to remind himself, for the rest of his life, that in order to preserve his desire to return to the Kingdoms, he had to keep his grief alive.

17

A Fleeting Glimpse

Iliån was discovering happiness.

They spent hours together, following one another in silence through the forest, or waiting in the branches for flocks of starlings. They encouraged the little puma to regain his liberty by bringing him to swim with them in the middle of the lake. For Iliån, whose childhood had been one of absolute solitude, Oliå's presence was revelatory. He didn't even need to glance at her to realize how his inner world had opened out to be twice as wide, twice as gentle. Yet he was also aware of the occasional shadows that passed across Oliå's face.

"The water is clear here," he said to her.

"So it is."

"It's the stream from the source that flows into the lake."

There was no response from Oliå, who was swimming ahead of him.

"Can you feel how cold it is?"

She dived beneath the crystalline waters to reach the warmer currents below.

Iliån knew that Oliå was a fairy. He had known from the very first instant, despite her talent for keeping her powers invisible and hiding them away among the ordinary mysteries of life. Whether it was a rain shower at an opportune moment, or a rock that jutted out just enough to offer them shelter, Iliån understood each of her gifts in turn. He had heard enough stories from his father, who had told him about the indomitable character of fairies; how they defied evil kings and wicked stepmothers. Oliå was like them, but she had something else too: a deep-set pain, a haunting woe, a secret that tugged at Iliån's heart.

Their happiness could have lasted forever. They were kindred spirits, both of them accustomed to a clandestine existence. They rarely spoke, preferring to listen to the wind and to breathe in the earth. Occasionally, when it was stormy, they would walk huddled together, leaning forward as though pushing at a wall of air and rain, before building huge fires to warm themselves again.

They would have had no difficulty staying hidden from the rest of the world; even the blood-soaked realm that besieged the forest and the lake had ceased to exist for them.

Returning late to the summer palace in a dreamlike state, Iliån took his father by the arm and lead him down to the pontoon.

"She's watching me," the king said.

Iliån stared around him in the darkness. His father saw the queen everywhere, in the red embers of a fire or the scuttling of a lizard. Tonight, the reflection on the water made it look as though there were two moons on the horizon, like a pair of open eyes.

"She's asleep on her bed. She's watching me."

On cloudy nights, or when the moon wasn't out, the king would whisper, "Let her sleep. It's fine. I made her wait for so long that I can easily hold out until morning."

He slowed his pace as if he didn't want to disturb the dark, before turning to look at the son he was unable to recognize.

"I will return alone on horseback. Away with you, boy. Your parents must be waiting."

Iliån knew that his father had long since ridden his

last horse, and formed his final cavalcade. Only the clouds, for their part, were galloping across the moon.

When he had accompanied his father back to his bedchamber, Iliån went to sit by Fåra's side.

"You come back a little later each day," the old man would comment, stitching a boot or carving pins out of little bird bones, as the water lapped at the stilts below them.

"I hope one day you don't come back at all."

Every time he would utter this phrase as though it were a prophecy, breaking off from his task to look at Iliån. Fåra was in no doubt that something had changed in the young prince's life.

One evening, his words sounded like an order.

"Life is not meant to be lived in a hole."

"This is no hole," Iliån answered for once. "And even if it were, I'm happy here."

"Think about the larvae that grow in the pontoon…"

Iliån watched Fåra's hands, which continued working delicately as he spoke.

"If the larvae do not leave their holes," said the servant, "they dry up like grains of barley and get eaten by the birds. You must leave before that happens to you, Majesty."

"What about you? What about my father?"

"We are too dry, too light for the birds."

"So what are you waiting for here?"

"The wind."

Iliån lay down on the floor and surveyed a star through the tattered straw roof. From the alcove came the sound of the king breathing on his bed.

"Don't worry about us any more," said the servant.

"Fåra…"

"I'm thinking about what your father would have wanted. About what your mother must be screaming in her silence. Go!"

"Fåra, I have to tell you…"

"I don't want to know."

"Why?"

Fåra looked at him solemnly.

"Don't let anyone bind you to these forests. You must leave them behind."

Iliån closed his eyes. Fåra had guessed at the secret love he was harbouring.

"You will soon be fifteen, the age when princes can become kings."

"I have no age. I don't exist."

"But your brother…"

"He has no reason to fear me. Doesn't my name

mean 'he who shall never reign'?"

"As far as Iån is concerned, you go by another name. One that will take his breath away when he finds out that you exist after all."

At that very instant, however, deep in the woods, King Iån was breathless for different reasons. It was the third time he had seen her.

The first time, two months earlier, she was crossing a bridge made of forest creepers high overhead. He had positioned himself in a crevice in the ground, and was lying in wait for two rebels that he and his archers had been pursuing for several days. The young king stayed on his own while the others scoured the banks of the lake. Suddenly, on seeing the bridge pull taut, he drew his dagger, only to discover that a young woman had appeared and was walking along, oblivious of his presence. It was a fleeting glimpse.

The second time, he wasn't there by accident. He had spent several long, sleepless weeks haunted by that vision. It was back in the same place on a misty day. He had to edge closer to get a better look at her face, causing her to vanish into the wispy fog before reaching the other side of the bridge. Afterwards, he took the captain of his archers into his confidence, charging him with finding out her name and the place where she lived, without breathing a word to Taåg or anyone else.

The captain's efforts had been in vain.

This, the third time, he'd managed to stay by her side for several minutes as she slept by a flickering fire. He hadn't needed anyone's help. The smell from the fire, mingled with his hunter's instincts, had drawn him towards her. It was cold. She slept wrapped in a green and gold cape that once upon a time must have been magnificent, but was now as worn as an old saddlecloth.

Her head was resting on the forest floor, and the light from the embers danced across her skin. He was right next to her, unable to move away: he found her truly dazzling. He wanted to be someone else, to wash the blood from his hands and be worthy of the enchanting soul he saw before him. He wanted her to feel no fear when she woke. For the first time, Iån felt the desire to look into a person's eyes and read something other than terror. But he did not disturb her, choosing instead to retreat over the moss, his heart pounding, the way one might recoil from a scorpion.

He went back to his horse, which he had left in a nearby thicket. He sought to numb himself by galloping all night across the hills, past roving families and the scorched remains of villages, causing the crows to fly from the fields. His disfigured land was like a mirror held up to his soul, and it drained him of all hope.

Iån returned to his castle at dawn. The squire who took his horse on the drawbridge told him that a man had been waiting for some time to see him. The king paid him no attention and climbed the stone stairs up to his apartments, which were plunged in darkness. He barricaded himself in there until evening, silencing anyone who knocked at his door.

When, at seven o'clock, he approached the window and drew the curtain aside, blinded by the evening light, he realized that he would give anything for the young girl. He would relinquish his power and hand over the keys of the realm to Tåag if he had to. He would lay down his weapons before her. He would abandon everything to share a corner of that cape, or to warm himself by that same fire out there in the depths of the wood.

At the next knock, he ordered the door to be opened.

His chief steward announced that Arån, the captain of his archers, had been requesting an audience since the previous day.

"I no longer require him."

His steward didn't dare insist, bowing to honour his master's wishes, but the captain had already appeared behind him.

"Majesty, allow me to speak with you."

The steward barred his entry.

"Get out," said Iån. "I succeeded without you."

"Majesty, you entrusted me with a mission."

"And now I am removing it from you."

"I found what you were looking for."

"I didn't wait for you."

Arån managed to barge his way up to the young king, who took out his dagger and pressed it against the captain's chest.

"I would keep my silence forever if my news were not worthy of your attention," whispered Arån.

The king slowly raised the blade towards his neck.

"In that case, I shall silence you myself."

He ordered the steward to leave, before turning back to the captain.

"Speak."

"I found the lady's trail again."

"I've already told you – you're too late."

"The trail leads to the source of the great lake."

"I know."

"The rain meant I could follow her tracks in the

mud. They always lead back to the source."

"I know all this, captain," said Iån. "You do not seem to hold your life dear…"

"Listen to me, Your Majesty."

The archer's dark stare made Iån retract his dagger slightly.

"Majesty, I must tell you… These footprints in the mud on the path come from the shore of the lake."

Iån didn't move.

"The shore," Arån tried again, "directly in front of the summer palace. The girl leaves the summer palace to go to the source."

The archer, like everyone else in the land, believed that the haunted palace was inhabited by an old king and his daughter. And that girl – provided she was alive and had not become a spectre roaming the waters – was Iån's sister.

The young king dropped his dagger, which buried itself in the floorboards. In the space of a few seconds, his burning love had frozen over.

She had killed his mother in childbirth. She had made his father lose his mind. And now she was murdering her brother, lifting up his heart only to shatter it more easily.

When Taåg entered the room later, newly arrived

from his marshlands, he did so in the knowledge that a new resolve had taken hold of his king. For the old genie had met the terror-stricken captain on the stone stairs.

Taåg lingered near the door, awaiting his order to enter.

"Leave me alone," said the king.

18

FLIGHT

The night was dark enough to lend her the courage to reveal her secret, but Oliå had been putting this moment off since the very first day.

She had just felt Iliån's hand come to rest on hers in the sand. Soon it would be too late.

"Wait..." she said.

They were sitting at the lakeside, surrounded by trees whose roots and trunks sank deep into the water.

In the daytime, it looked as if giants were wading across the lake on stilts; by night, it became a living labyrinth that enveloped its mysteries.

Before them on the water, Iliån saw the faint lights of the summer palace. He had just dared to touch her for the first time, and he wasn't sure he was bold enough for what was to follow.

"I need to tell you something," Oliå continued.

Iliån's hand stayed where it was. The forest hummed around them.

"I know," he ventured.

"No, you don't."

"I know about your powers."

She sighed. For her, there were no powers. How she wished that was the only thing she had to tell him. Yes, she was a fairy: that in itself was enough to make both of them weep.

Had it been just that, they would have begrudged time for gradually separating them from each other, for leaving Oliå to her youth while Iliån grew older. The tears might have consoled them in the end. They would have held each other tight, their feet in the water. And they would have told each other that nothing would make them afraid, that nothing could tear them apart.

"The queen died because I blocked the source."

These words from Oliå swooped down on Iliån, attacking him so suddenly that he didn't even hear them.

"I blocked the source and the lake dried up."

Now her voice was starting to register.

"It was Taåg… He forced me to keep the source closed until your birth. He said that if I refused, he would contaminate the lake forever with mud from his swamps."

Oliå spoke with difficulty, dragging each word from her heart like thorns, or birds that had been nesting there for too long.

"I did it for the queen and for you... I was the guardian of the source. I wanted you to grow up with clean water."

She had to catch her breath between each admission.

"But by the time I had smashed through the dry clay with a stone, and the water came back ... it was too late."

Silence from next to her. The only sound was the nocturnal hum of the lake.

She didn't tell him how she had taken care of him throughout his childhood; how she had lived in hiding but run across the water every single evening to stand guard before the palace; how she had watched over the prince while he slept. It was her way of mending her mistake. She chased away the raiders who approached in their boats, enveloping them with swarms of fireflies and capsizing their vessels with armies of catfish. In the end, rumours abounded that the palace was ringed by evil forces.

This time it was Oliå's turn to move her hand

towards Iliån's, but he had disappeared. In the distance, on the other side of the lake, she saw a shadow climb up one of the stilts and stop in front of the summer palace's main lantern.

Iliån, just out of the water, turned back in her direction, but all he could see was the dark smudge of the trees. Sadness and anger overwhelmed him. Shivering in the cold, he felt as if the recent months had been nothing but a betrayal. How could she have let him believe in happiness when she had been responsible for destroying his life?

If he had been left with hatred alone, Iliån could have recovered. He would have cursed the girl-spirit who had deceived him and the trust he had placed in her. But the worst was that, through the pain, he could feel his love intact. He was ashamed of it. There wasn't even the smallest dent in this mad love of his. He adored Oliå just as he had the first day. But now he had left, and he'd never be able to return.

Fåra appeared behind him on the pontoon.

"My prince?"

Iliån turned to see the servant prostrated before his feet.

He held out a hand to help the old man up.

"What is it, Fåra?"

The prince didn't have the strength for yet another ordeal.

"They came for you," said the old servant.

"Who?"

"Your brother, Iån, and his men."

"My brother..."

Iliån dashed inside the palace and crossed the room towards his father's bed, where he found the king with his head swathed in a white bandage. Kneeling at his side, the young prince clasped his father's lukewarm hand.

"He's still alive. Go. I will watch over him," said Fåra, who had followed him in.

"What did they do to him?"

"He hurled himself at the guards who were trying to search the queen's former bedchamber. Two others rebuffed him and he hit his head on the bed. They're looking for you."

The king had opened his blue eyes, which darted across the tattered canopy above, then closed again.

"My prince," Fåra begged, "leave us. I will take care of everything. They will come back. You still have a chance to escape."

Iliån felt tears pricking at his eyes.

"You can run away. In the old days there was a

ferryman at the edge of the salt marshes. Grab your chance: they don't know who you are."

Fåra continued in hushed tones, "They're looking for a girl. Your brother thinks he has a sister. He told me so."

"A sister?" Iliån repeated.

The old man sifted through his memory.

"Everyone was expecting a princess. Thinking back, I remember the doctors announcing it before your birth."

The servant's face brightened.

"That is why they won't find you."

Iliån had never heard this story before. In her dying moments, was it possible that even his mother had been unaware she'd given birth to a son?

"Go towards the sea," Fåra said. "Seek out the ferryman beyond the salt marshes. Iån and his men went the other way."

The prince looked at his father, then back at Fåra. For the first time, he was genuinely considering leaving. Perhaps this was what his mother would have urged him to do. Her death must not be in vain.

He thought of Oliå.

There was nothing more to bind Iliån to this land.

"Iån wants you dead. He came here to kill you."

"When did they arrive?"

"As night was falling."

Iliån stood up. He had never been as far as the sea, but Fåra had spoken to him before of the ferryman and of the marshes that ended in sand and shells.

"Right now," Fåra continued, "they ought to be at the source. You must leave."

He carried on, almost with a smile, refusing to acknowledge Iliån's distraught face.

"They'll be looking for a girl up there, by which time you'll be far—"

"Fåra, what did you just say?" the young prince murmured.

"You'll have several hours' head start on them."

"My brother spoke of the source?"

"Yes…"

"A girl … by the source of the lake?"

Fåra turned deathly pale: what had he said that was so terrible?

Iliån fled the palace and dived into the dark water. He swam to the sandy shore, which was still churned up from the men's boots. He ran into the woods, crashing straight through the mesh of brambles, lianas and hawthorns without once altering his course, leaving behind a trail of blood and clothing.

The night sky had brightened, and he made no attempt to hide as he drew near the source. He cried out her name, throwing himself into the pool where the water reached his chest.

"Oliå! Oliå!"

He stopped.

A little way off, the puma seemed to be sleeping on the bank, a paw rocking in the flow of the water.

"Oliå!"

Iliån felt his hope restored, and bounded down the little waterfall that was glowing white beneath the moon. Perhaps Oliå was even further downstream, where any sound of voices would be drowned out by the rapids.

But when he stroked the animal's fur with his hand, he felt the criss-cross of two arrows between his fingers. The puma must have been killed as it reared up in the air, since the arrow tips had struck him on his back, near the neck. He had leapt to defend his mistress, only to be pierced mid-flight by two archers positioned below.

Iliån waded back upstream. The irises were still there, just as they had been the first time, but Oliå's glistening hands were no longer laying stones. There was nobody.

FLIGHT

As the secret prince returned to the place where the source sprang from the hillside, he thought he heard a distant roar. Then he collapsed onto the moss.

19

UNDER THE ALMOND TREES

JOSHUA ILIÅN PEARL DIDN'T RETURN TO PARIS straight away.

He spent his first six months in a village in Provence, in the free zone of southern France, avoiding the occupied territories to the north of the country: he was afraid that the German secret police would be waiting for him outside *Maison Pearl*, so he needed to lie low following his escape.

Joshua arrived at the home of Thérèse Pilon on the first Sunday in March. As he walked up the wide path that led to the house, he felt as if the almond trees were bursting into blossom before his very eyes. The weather was glorious, and the trunks seemed to be twisting in every direction, straining to reach the sun.

He had only been here once before: between two

overnight train journeys, during his first winter in this world.

The Pilon farm had been *Maison Pearl*'s sole supplier of almonds going as far back as the 1890s. The marshmallows with almond flakes had been all the rage in Paris for decades: it was said that the cook of a famous politician bought a kilo at the beginning of each month, and Madame Pearl swore she'd seen the legendary actor Jean Gabin come in for a whole batch, disguised as a chauffeur so as not to be recognized.

From that day on, Monsieur Pearl liked to tease his wife about all the customers who crossed their threshold, joking that they were the ghost of Queen Victoria masquerading as a cobbler or a kitchen maid. But that only made Esther Pearl all the more adamant about the time she'd seen Gabin larger than life on the silver screen.

"I watched him at the Louxor-Pathé. You're just jealous! You should have more faith in us ladies when it comes to remembering the face of a handsome gentleman…"

So it was that one winter's day, Jacques Pearl had sent Joshua south to fetch an extra crate of almonds, just in case they fell short ahead of the Christmas rush.

It had been Joshua's first trip out of Paris. Racing

through the countryside, he had discovered the magic of travelling by train and the beauty of the almond trees on the snow-covered hillsides.

Now, two years later in February 1942, on crossing the border back into France after his time in captivity, the farm had immediately sprung to mind as a place of refuge.

Through her window, Thérèse Pilon recognized the visitor striding up through the cloud of blossom. She put the kettle on the stove and went to stand in the sunshine by the door.

"If you've come for almonds, you'll have to wait a while yet."

The young man was twenty metres from her, by the well. She spoke loudly, gesturing towards the fields of almond trees: it was early March, and the flowers would not be bearing their fruit until summer.

But Madame Pilon could tell instantly that the boy hadn't come for almonds. She motioned at him to sit on the stone step; then she disappeared, returning with two cups of chicory coffee.

He still hadn't said a word when she sat down next to him.

"They're late finishing the vines down there – would you like to help with the pruning over the next few days? Then, in a month, there'll be all the work you could wish for: they might call this the 'free zone', but it's war down here just like up there."

"Are you alone?" he asked, looking around him.

Thérèse leant towards him and fluttered her eyelids as if he'd just asked for her hand in marriage.

"What about you?" she enquired tenderly.

Joshua smiled in embarrassment as she started giggling like an eight-year-old girl.

Thérèse Pilon had lost her husband a quarter of a century earlier in the Great War, when she was several months pregnant and still a very young woman.

When the mayor's wife, dressed in black, came to give her the news, Thérèse had sent her packing, calling her a liar. She had prayed day and night for her husband to return: heaven would not betray her faith. She could feel the baby she was expecting inside her, more alive than ever.

So she did what an old aunt had taught her to do when she was little, and she drew three figures under an almond tree on a square of paper, then took it to the church and slid it beneath the statue of Saint Joseph. Ask and you shall receive.

She believed this act would be her salvation. Three. That was the image she'd had of her little family, ever since falling pregnant. Two parents and a healthy child. It also meant three pairs of hands for working the land, which should be just enough for the struggle with nature.

But the following day, they brought her husband's body in a coffin, and a flag and a drummer accompanied the pregnant young widow to the cemetery.

Railing at God and his saints, Thérèse Pilon turned her back on the drawing under the statue. Yet when spring came, she gave birth to twins: two sons, both with eyes the colour of almonds. So in the end, she did have her family of three, just as it was represented in the little sketch yellowing in the chapel.

"Where are they?" asked Joshua, looking at Thérèse.

"They're out walking. Trying to get away from all the girls, who are constantly after them. I liked it better before."

She smiled, burying her nose in her cup.

And so, for a while, Joshua became the fourth figure under the almond tree. He and the boys, who were a little older than him, were inseparable. The three of them worked hard during the day, and then the twins would down tools and head out for the evening.

Joshua would stay in with Thérèse Pilon and talk through his plans. He still hadn't written to the Pearls, fearing that any correspondence would be intercepted; but he worried about them, despite Thérèse's attempts to console him.

Initially, the three boys worked for the neighbours down in the valley, after which everyone came to help them gather the first almonds. This June harvest produced flat almonds with a sappy taste.

It was then that Thérèse Pilon received an order from *Maison Pearl*. She showed it to Joshua as though it were a keenly awaited postcard, even though the only words written on the blue paper were:

Two kilos of unshelled almonds still in their green hulls, please, Madame Pilon.
Regards.
Pearl

Joshua recognized the order, which was typical for the month of June, since they needed this first crop of slightly bitter almonds in order to prepare a special type of marshmallow, that would be sold until the end of summer.

This sign of life put his mind at rest. Incredible though it seemed, *Maison Pearl* was standing firm in the great winds of war, surviving from season to season despite all manner of persecution. Thérèse Pilon had reassured him that the Pearls weren't under any threat: marshmallows were neither Jews nor collaborators nor communists. Their only allegiance was to sugar.

For Joshua Pearl, that summer was almost carefree. He learnt how to use a bicycle and rode along the country roads, stopping beneath the plane trees or exploring the local villages in the sultry afternoons when everything shut down. The free zone that spanned half of southern France was under the authority of a government that took its orders from Germany, but the shadow of occupation loomed large. The Pilon family had introduced Joshua as a cousin from the north, and Thérèse told her sons to call him Jo so that his full name remained hidden. The French police were on the lookout for Jews living in the free zone, and Cousin Joshua, with that unplaceable accent of his, wouldn't escape their notice.

The main almond harvest took place in September, and half the village turned out to help the Pilon family. The men shook the branches with batons several metres long and the women gathered the fruit as it fell to the ground, placing it in sacks. They would form a line and spin round the tree like the hand of a clock, teasing the lazy women who bagged the spot nearest the trunk, because they'd only have to take three steps each turn.

When the work was done, they spent joyous evenings in the house, drinking sweet wine as they removed the green hulls. People of all ages squeezed onto benches in the main room, the boys making discreet decisions about which girl to work alongside, while some of the women sang.

An old man told stories that tugged at Jo Pearl's heartstrings. Each of the tales was familiar to him, and even the voice of the storyteller reminded him of his father's. The man spoke of a blue beard, of a wood-cutter, of a little girl and some matches, and of a fairy godmother who could make carriages spring from pumpkins.

Pearl looked into the gleaming eyes of everybody there and sensed that all was not lost. A wicked spell had banished him to this world in order to erase his past, and yet he was finding that past everywhere: in the voice of an old man and the gaze of a child. His memory of the Kingdoms always seemed to be awoken on resonant occasions: a happy or solemn moment, a small gathering next to a fire or a profound conversation as night was falling, was all it took for the window to open ever so slightly. Pearl simply needed to find a way of stepping through it.

In the days that followed the harvest, he spent hours in the room where the fruit was laid out to dry. The entire space was filled thirty centimetres high with the almonds in their shells. They rose up to Joshua's knees as he ploughed them with his feet, walking slowly back and forth to turn them over, all the while feeling as though he were wading through a stream. The scent of marzipan made his head spin.

He had kept the second little note from *Maison Pearl* that had been sent at the start of July, confirming safe receipt of the delivery. On the back of the sheet, Jacques Pearl had already outlined the details of the next order for autumn.

Joshua adored the intricate handwriting beneath the pearl-studded crown of the shop's emblem. He missed Madame Pearl's voice, too, and he vowed that he would return to spend the winter in Paris and in that shop. It was the only place on earth that felt like home to him.

At the end of October, well ahead of schedule, they sent off the order, with a few little cakes and dried figs thrown in as a present. It filled three very heavy crates, and Joshua Pearl felt a pang of desire to stash himself inside and travel with the cargo.

Barely a week later, on the first day of the olive

harvest, Thérèse Pilon came back from the village to find all three crates in front of the well, with two words painted over the crossed-out names of Jacques and Esther Pearl.

PERSONS UNKNOWN

The delivery had been returned to the Pilon farm.

Thérèse started running, leaving the dusty path to cut between the green oaks. She could hear the sound of voices and laughter in the distance. She clambered over a stone wall into a field of olive trees, where Joshua was working with some other pickers. He was the first to see her coming.

She walked up to him and spoke into his ear.

He dropped his bucket, and the olives spilled out onto the grass.

20

THE BLUE SLIPPER

It took him several days to reach Paris. He made the train journey in short stages, only choosing cargo wagons. As stealthy as if he were back in the world of his childhood, he reached the occupied zone via forest tracks. Then he borrowed a bicycle to continue his journey north, sleeping in the hay lofts of farms or the tool sheds of cemeteries.

Finally, he reached Paris on the rainy evening of 10 November 1942.

Standing in front of *Maison Pearl*, he was confronted with the lowered iron shutter. He tried to take some reassurance from the other closed shops around him: the street was deserted, blotted out by the rain. The lowered shutter didn't mean anything at all. Perhaps the shopkeepers had closed up a little earlier than usual? After all, 11 November was still

Armistice Day, even if the occupying army had for-bidden the locals to celebrate the anniversary of the German defeat in 1918.

As he stepped out of the rain, Joshua noticed a vertical inscription on the window's wooden frame.

He tilted his head to read it:

Pearls to swine!

Another hand had clearly used some wire wool in an attempt to erase this malicious message.

Joshua retreated to the opposite pavement, to the exact spot where he had stood in the rain when Jacques Pearl had come to his rescue all those years ago. It was pelting down almost as hard as it had been that night.

Where were they? What had happened over the last few months? Suddenly, he looked up at the window of the Pearls' apartment and saw a very faint glimmer of light peeking through a gap in the curtains. There was hope! They were hiding inside; they were all right after all.

Joshua skirted round the side of the building, pushed the door open and raced up the stairs. He tried to detect the scent of roasting lamb, or thyme, or potato gratin, hoping for any aroma to float down the steps; but the stairwell only smelt of rat poison.

On the landing, he pounded at the door and waited. After several more knocks, he thought he heard a little noise on the other side, though it might have been the sound of his heart pounding beneath his coat. He went down two steps, slipped his hand into a hatch that was used for checking the lead pipes, and retrieved a key. Returning to the door he thrust the key into the lock, but it came up against another key that prevented him from turning it: the door was locked from the inside.

He slid down against the door in resignation.

A few minutes later, Joshua walked down Rue de Saintonge and stopped outside number 24. This was where the plasterer and his daughters lived; where, as a younger man, he had spent his final Christmas Eve before the war.

In the stairwell, he met the youngest daughter, Colette, who burst into tears when she saw him. Unable to speak, she took his arm and led him up to the second floor. They were greeted by a tremendous silence. The whole family was sitting around the table, and the two older daughters looked at Joshua as though he were a ghost. The father stood up and shook his hand.

"Where are they?"

The plasterer couldn't answer; instead it was his wife, appearing behind his shoulder, who spoke on her husband's behalf.

"It's been several months now. The police came for them back in August. They'd rounded up the others the previous month, almost every shopkeeper in the neighbourhood. Four families went from our building alone."

"Where are they?"

"Nobody knows."

The father tried to speak, but again without success. His wife translated for him.

"My husband went to the town hall and to the police headquarters three times to ask where they were. The butcher's daughter was best friends with our youngest girl."

Colette was still sobbing behind Joshua, but it was the eldest, Suzanne, sitting bolt upright on her chair, who was the most overwhelmed to see him again.

"You have to go into hiding," urged the mother, when Joshua didn't appear to believe what they were telling him.

"Do you have somewhere you can go?" asked Suzanne.

"I saw a light."

"Where?"

"At their apartment."

"My boy…" the plasterer sighed.

"Someone's there."

"No," said the woman, "no one's there any more."

"I promise you I saw a light."

The man took Joshua by the shoulder and held him tight.

"Where can you go?" asked the plasterer's wife again.

"There's someone in their apartment."

"I'll take him there," said Suzanne, standing up. "We'll have a look around and then I'll come back."

Her parents let them go, since it was still ahead of curfew hour. Suzanne grabbed a woollen shawl from the hallway, and Joshua followed her out.

As they walked side by side down the street, Joshua glanced under her umbrella and noticed that her face had become that of an older woman, at just seventeen. War makes you grow up fast.

They arrived in front of the shop and stared up at the windows on the first floor. As night fell, the rain was coming down more heavily than ever.

No light was coming through the curtains.

They pushed open the side door and headed up the main stairs until they reached the Pearls' landing, where Joshua removed the key from his pocket. The lock worked perfectly. He froze.

"Just now, it was locked from the inside."

"Perhaps the key fell out on the other side," said Suzanne.

They entered the apartment and Joshua groped around in the dark, trying to find whether the other key had indeed dropped onto the floor. Nothing. The whole place was pitch black: the electricity wasn't working.

"Look."

Suzanne had found some matches and two candles in a drawer in the hallway, and they walked from room to room by candlelight. Everything was in perfect order, with the beds made and the dishes clean. And yet Suzanne remembered how the arrest had taken place at dawn on a bright summer's day. Joshua was shivering, his hair soaked through from the rain, as he leant towards a photo of Jacques and Esther Pearl on their wedding day. The plasterer's daughter seemed as moved as the young man.

"My father spoke to Monsieur Pearl, who told him that you were in a camp in Germany. They should have used that in their favour to stay alive. The families of prisoners don't get touched."

When she saw that he hadn't reacted, she added, "But Pearl said it would've been dishonest, because you weren't officially their son."

Joshua shook his head in the half-light.

"So who are you if you aren't their son? Maybe you aren't Jewish? Maybe you can stay with us."

Joshua knew it was too late. And yet he didn't regret choosing to take on the name of Joshua Pearl on the brink of war, even if it was akin to turning himself into game bird on the morning of a shoot.

"I saw a light in here," he said.

He ran his fingers over the furniture and didn't find a single speck of dust.

"I could run away with you," said Suzanne, staring at Joshua's hands on the wood.

He turned towards her.

"I want to run away with you," she repeated, her back pressed against the sitting room window.

When he saw that she was crying he took a step towards her, but his foot caught a stray object on the carpet. He bent down and picked it up: it was a woman's shoe, a sort of blue-leather ballet pump. Madame Pearl's foot would never have fitted into such a slipper, not in a million years.

"Is this yours?" he asked.

"No."

He'd already forgotten about Suzanne's tears and his impulse to move towards her. He kept turning the shoe over in his hands.

"Maybe it belongs to the girl who worked in the shop," she said.

Joshua recalled how the letter he'd received from Jacques Pearl in the prison camp had mentioned a young girl.

"What was her name?" he asked.

"Léa."

"Did she live here?"

"No."

"Where is she?"

"She must have been taken with them. She used to arrive at the shop very early; that's it, she'll have been taken with them."

Joshua remembered the photograph of *Maison Pearl* with the small, faint footprints in the snow. Yes, this slipper might belong to Léa. He thought of all the footprints that had been erased for ever, and he placed the blue slipper in his pocket.

"If they find you with me," he said to Suzanne, as the water coursed down the window behind her, "they'll take you too. Anyway, listen: this is no time to be running away."

"And what about you?" asked Suzanne. "Where will you go?"

Joshua didn't answer, but turned round to take one last look at the little apartment before they left. He double-locked the door and replaced the key in its hiding place.

He accompanied Suzanne back to Rue Saintonge, but he didn't want to go upstairs.

"At least let me watch you leave," she said, stoically holding her folded umbrella against her. "After that, I'll go up to join my parents."

And so he set off through the puddles, without once turning around.

A few buildings along, sheltered in a doorway, another young girl was watching him. She stood barefoot on the pavement, and in one hand she clasped a blue shoe.

Without realizing it, Joshua had stolen her other blue slipper, the one that had fallen off her left foot when she'd jumped backwards to hide in the folds of the curtains. The same slipper that had checked Joshua's movement towards Suzanne.

21

Until the Fighting is Over

When Joshua Pearl crossed the demarcation line into the free zone, heading back towards his refuge in Provence, there were hundreds of tanks on his heels, as well as the stamping of thousands of pairs of boots. So bitter was his sense of loss that he had no idea this day, 11 November 1942, had been chosen by Hitler to invade the south in order to occupy France in its entirety.

He arrived, his hands in his pockets, on the night of a full moon. The earth had been tilled between the trees.

In the distance, he had just spotted the roof of the Pilon farm with its undulating tiles, when two shadows pinned him to the ground and bundled him into the ditch. A voice hissed at him not to move. Doors slammed close to the house and a car started up, driving along the track right next to them.

"That's the police," the voice informed him.

Joshua finally recognized his assailant. It was one of the Pilon twins with a bandit's scarf around his face.

"We've been waiting for you for four nights," said the other man. "I'm glad that's over. Welcome."

Joshua was black and blue from his tumble and didn't recognize this second grinning shadow, who was holding out a hand to help him up from the mud.

"They came for you the day after your departure," the man explained. "Someone had turned you in to the police, and they searched the house and found the weapons."

"What weapons?" asked Joshua.

"Ours."

In these few sentences whispered in the ditch, Joshua was discovering that the twins were not the same men he thought he'd known. For a long time now, they'd been part of the secret army preparing to liberate the country. And the young women called Constance or Juliette who took up their nights, the ones Thérèse Pilon used to complain about so frequently, were in fact the secret code names of resistance operations.

By chance, when the police had come to the farm, the twins were on a windy mistral-swept hilltop, preparing for an act of sabotage. They had been warned just in time not to return to the farm, and had set themselves up in the scrubland. From there, they organized a secret resistance movement, known as the *maquis*. They hadn't even had a chance to say goodbye to their mother, who was left on her own with her almond trees.

Jo Pearl was greeted as a brother in arms by the ten or so men who lived between the shepherds' huts dotted across the high plateaux of Provence.

Their leader went by the name of "Captain Alexandre". He was tall and thickset. When Joshua was presented to him, he was working at a table in a corner, next to a window that overlooked a small drinking fountain. On the lime wash wall, Alexandre had pinned a photo of a small and very old painting: it depicted a woman shining a candle for a traveller.

"What's your name?"

"Pearl."

Joshua was staring at the picture, which was luminous as a flame.

"You need to find a *nom de guerre*. Nobody here keeps his name from before," said Captain Alexandre, his pencil hovering over an open notebook. "We all assume a combatant name. Where are you from?"

"Somewhere very far away."

Alexandre smiled at the man standing three paces from him, and jotted a few lines in his sloping handwriting. Pearl could only make out three words: *grief* and *crystal clear*.

"Well? What will your name be?"

"Iliån."

"Do you have a sweetheart?"

Iliån didn't answer, but his eyes had lit up.

"Her name?"

"Oliå."

He hadn't said her name out loud for the longest time.

"She won't get in the way of my work," Iliån reassured the captain, who was staring at him.

"You mustn't see her, or talk to her. We're all soldiers and monks here until the fighting is over."

"I promise. I won't see her."

The fighting lasted for nearly three years. Iliån found himself at the heart of this invisible army, which spun its web from the mountains all the way to the sea. He kept hidden, spied on traitors, blew up enemy cars, lit night fires so that weapons could be parachuted in. He never left any trace behind, and he changed shelter as soon as darkness fell. He was a cicada by day and a cricket by night. In winter, he reverted to the white hare of his childhood, becoming once more the elusive animal who disappeared in the snow.

He was often alone, and took his orders from messages slipped into his hand in some corner of a wood. It was rare for him to see his companions, and rarer still to see Alexandre.

And yet he had never forgotten a particular encounter with the captain. One night, they had both spent hours listening out for the throbbing of a plane that never came. They were expecting cylinders full of weapons to be dropped in a lavender field. Joshua was sitting on his heels, perfectly still, not batting an eyelid. He could hear the breathing of the captain when he placed his revolver in front of him.

There were long periods of silence between them. When Alexandre finally spoke, Joshua felt as if his leader had been reading his thoughts all the while. Each word bored a tunnel into him and shone a light down it.

"Remind me of that name again."

"What name?"

"Your sweetheart's."

Silence.

"Oliå."

"Are you thinking about her right now?"

"No."

"Why not?"

Iliån didn't answer.

"You should try to imagine what she's doing."

"I don't want to."

"Everything starts from that. And life comes just behind. It follows the imagination with fierce loyalty."

Around them, the night was quiet and still.

"When the world is ready to understand that," he said, "when the world is ready to really believe…"

In the dark, the rustling of his sleeve betrayed a sweeping gesture: a gesture to indicate war.

"…We'll stop all of this. And you'll find your Oliå again."

Could he hear Joshua Pearl's secrets, simmering away?

"But nobody's ready to believe yet," Alexandre went on. "They must have tokens of proof, do you understand? Proof."

Joshua was surrendering to the resonance of these words, which made him feel less alone.

"They must have tokens of proof."

The plane didn't come; no weapons landed on the long rows of lavender. When day broke, they went their separate ways.

But for Pearl, that night was a moment of illumination. Taåg had consigned him to exile in this world. Rather than trying to find the way out, he should change this world and its reluctance to believe in the stories from the Kingdoms. Doubt was his prison: he could only break free from it by finding tokens of proof. That's what would reverse the spell and return him to where he came from.

Iliån would find these tokens. He would collect them one by one. In the meantime, he had to survive.

Occasionally, there were betrayals. Captain Alexandre used to say that war had turned him into a monster of justice. Even the most righteous battles have their monstrous aspect.

Above all, Iliån experienced the tiny miracles that embellish lives given to a cause, to fighting the great battles.

Joshua Pearl woke up one day in a country at peace. The enemy had been conquered, and American soldiers began to arrive. Their tanks suddenly resembled carnival floats, with jubilant crowds trailing after them. They handed out cigarettes and chewing gum.

Joshua was present at the reunion of Thérèse Pilon and her sons. Standing back a little, hat in hand, he was very moved by their fervent embraces. They made an effort to include him in their celebrations, but he knew there was now one person too many under the almond trees.

The next day, he decided to leave while the house was still asleep. He got dressed in the farmhouse kitchen. There was a small parcel on the table, and on it was written:

Iliàn

He picked up the package. Someone had guessed that he was about to leave. He didn't open it, but tucked the object in his bag as a little treat for later.

As he left, he grabbed a fistful of almonds from a tree to complete his provisions. It was 20 August 1944. Two hours later, he witnessed the columns of liberators on the road. Children were sitting astride the tanks' guns; he climbed up as if he were hopping on a bus, and spent three days heading back up north amid the festive atmosphere.

It was at the gates of Paris, which would be liberated the following day, that Joshua Pearl finally thought to open the little package.

He immediately recognized the cord and leather

pouch that had been wrapped in a page torn from a notebook. Instantly, all the commotion around him dimmed. All he could hear was a muffled hubbub.

In his hands was the slingshot from his childhood; the one he had never been without, until that final night when he had been banished from the Kingdoms. An object from home had just joined him in exile.

And inside the wrapping, on paper with blue lines, there were six words in a childish hand that was round and careful. Six words stolen from Captain Alexandre:

They must have tokens of proof.

22

SORCERESS

"Who have you locked in the glass chamber?" asked Taåg, suddenly bursting into the corridor of the armoury.

The captain of the archers was walking swiftly to catch up with old Taåg.

"Has His Majesty spoken to you?" Arån asked.

"No."

All Taåg knew was that they had captured someone near the source of the lake. He felt increasingly distanced from the king's confidence. After being ostracized for three years for opposing Iån's schemes, he had resumed his place at the young king's side; but he had never truly regained the power that had been bestowed on him at the beginning of his godson's reign.

"Who is in the chamber?" he repeated.

Arån was well aware of Taåg's powers, and knew

better than to make an enemy of him.

"I threw a wounded lioness in there," replied the archer to cover his tracks. "We'd seen her change form three times before we captured her."

"Who is she?"

"First a weasel, then a bird, then a lioness. What she is now I'm not sure. The king himself doesn't know her name," said Arån, quickening his step. His whole body was soaking wet from the storm he had just confronted. Outside, a powerful wind was whipping up the sea and bending the cedars. He had inspected the fortifications, as far as the point where they petered out on the wild coast, but the hurricane remained at the castle's doors. Archers passed up and down the corridors carrying torches, and around them the thick walls of the armoury were lined with metal and weapons.

"Let me go up to the glass chamber," Taåg said.

"I have orders not to allow anyone to enter."

"Those orders don't concern me."

"I seem to remember that in the past, it wasn't your decision whether you went up there or not..."

Taåg shuddered. He had spent the terrible, isolated years of his confinement in the uppermost reaches of the winter castle, a captive in that chamber where magical powers were sent into disarray. He'd almost been driven mad between those glass walls, the very ones that had been built on his instruction to lock up unruly genies.

"I will obey my king if he orders me to bring you up," said Arån. "Be patient."

Four men approached them as a metal gate creaked open, and Taåg was pushed aside by a stream of archers.

Arån and his troop climbed high up the dark tower, where the air was all the cooler with the altitude. The twisting stairway seemed never-ending, and the wind played it like a pan flute. Through the arrow slits in the pumice stone, birds could be seen battling the squall outside. Arån ordered his men to stay at the top of the stairs as he entered alone to join the king.

Once the door swung shut, silence descended.

In front of him, the young king was standing before a vast glass structure, a perfect cube, in the centre of the room.

The glass walls were divided into a patchwork of irregular small panels with soldered edges, like stained-glass windows. There was a layer of mercury trapped between the panes, which meant that anyone on the outside of the chamber could see in, while the captives – prevented from seeing out – were faced with a myriad of their own reflections.

Arån didn't notice Oliå straight away, and for a moment he thought the king was gazing into an empty box. Then, as he approached the glass wall, he finally saw her.

She was sitting in a corner of the chamber which she hoped was a blind spot. An exhausted Oliå had been locked up in the dead of night and, huddling into that spot, had immediately fallen asleep to forget the nightmare of the chase.

The previous evening, at the source, the white puma had been the first to detect the presence of Iån and his archers. Crouching close to the ground, Oliå had heard the beast collapse at the side of the stream. The archers had seen the girl emerge next to the source, and she would have been shot through from all angles had the king not intervened to tell them to take her alive.

But when she instantly transformed herself into a weasel and disappeared into the brambles, the king realized that the odds were against them, and he changed his mind.

Dead or alive. That was the new order.

A hail of arrows beseiged Oliå as she climbed a tree trunk and leapt into the neighbouring branches. She had spent a long time as a weasel when she had wanted to shun her human form, after the queen's death. She knew by heart how to use her tail as a balancing pole, and how to taper her body to slice through the air. Now she was flying across the tree-tops in the darkness.

But these were the best archers in all the land, each one with a quiver on his back that held two hundred arrows. They ran beneath the branches, eyes trained upwards and fingers drawing their bowstrings taut. With every leap, she could feel the sharp tips brushing past her fur. She had made the wind blow unpredictably, which disrupted the arrows' flight and helped her to glide. But when a fresh volley nearly pinned her against the bark of a tree, she realized that her time as a weasel was coming to an end. Dodging the arrows, she slipped below a branch covered in ferns and emerged as a swallow, before darting up into the night sky. Seconds later, she would have been high above the clouds, touching the stars, but she never had the chance: an arrow whistled through the air and broke her wing.

At first, Oliå span round on herself, hanging in mid-air, too stunned to react, the forest, lake and red horizon flashing before her as the arrows continued to streak past.

In years gone by, she had been a hummingbird, a frog or a butterfly at the mercy of children, but never before had she felt so vulnerable. The advantage of the eternal youth that was ruining her life was that it had kept her safe from fear.

That night, as fear overwhelmed her for the first time, she understood that something had changed. What was happening? A new sensation was coursing through her tiny feathered body as it tumbled to the ground. Meeting Iliån had sparked a revolution inside her.

She felt vulnerable. And this discovery emboldened her as she plummeted like a stone in the night. The branches of the trees broke her fall. Just as she reached the dark undergrowth, her shadow started to expand, and her new feline body rolled across the blanket of dead leaves. She stood up. The wound she'd sustained as a swallow was still throbbing, but now it was on the front paw of a lioness. She bore another wound, too: the one left by Iliån when he had abandoned her at the lakeside.

Oliå purred. She could already hear the archers' cries as they went on with their search. She disappeared into the darkness, treading carefully on her paw before stopping to lick the wound. The voices seemed to be heading further away.

Suddenly, the lioness looked up to see Iån right in front of her. She froze. The king glared. From a nearby thicket came the sound of rustling and heavy breathing, and then a net swooped down on her. She was in too much distress to change one last time into a rat or a grain of pollen. Even Iliån, far in the distance, could hear her desperate roar. Oliå let them carry her off.

Back in the high tower, Arån and the king were now watching this young girl of fifteen. She had ripped up the men's clothes she'd been thrown, draping them over her like sheets to keep out the cold. From inside this glass chamber, it was impossible to imagine the storm that was shaking the realm.

Iån had placed a sword in a scarlet scabbard on the stone floor before him.

Arån understood why he had been summoned. He had just completed his tenth year serving his master, carrying out all the king's most sinister tasks: he would have had no hesitation in killing himself had he received the order to do so. But something told him he wouldn't be able to stomach this new mission.

The archer took a gamble.

"Is there any precedent of this in Your Majesty's lineage?"

"Precedent of what?"

"A fairy."

Iån remained silent. He was well aware that fairies were descended from fairies, so it was impossible for his own sister to be one.

"We must question the old servant from the summer palace," Arån continued. "I can bring him here. He will be able to recognize if it's her."

"No. Stay with me. There's no fairy here."

The king's eyes never left Olia.

"Sorcery has possessed her. She was born stained from the blood of her first crime, and she grew up with that guilt. How can she not be cursed? Where do you see a fairy? This is a sorceress."

That description seemed to bear no resemblance to what Arån was witnessing through the glass: a creature more gentle, more pure, more radiant than he had ever seen in his life. There was indeed sorcery in the air, but no hint of any curse.

"Take my sword," said the king.

The girl was resting her hand on her wounded shoulder, and in places her white skin had burn marks from the chase. She must have been cold beneath the rags, but she refused to dress herself more warmly.

"Taåg…" the archer said suddenly. "Taåg can tell whether she's a sorceress."

This time, Iån wavered.

Arån awaited the verdict with his eyes closed. How would he find the strength to pick up the sword, enter the chamber, watch her clutch the scraps of cloth a little more tightly, as she tried to guess the intention of the armed man advancing towards her? How could he bear to look into her eyes as he raised the weapon?

"I have no faith in Taåg," said the king. "Take my sword and kill her."

Arån started to talk in a way he would never have dared to before.

"Permit me to speak out of turn as a mere soldier, Majesty," the captain continued, amazed he was still alive after such insolence. "But I have watched you ever since you began the search for this young girl. If there's any chance—"

"That's enough, Arån."

"If there's any chance that no bloodline—"

Iån leant forward and drew his sword from its scabbard, but Arån stood firm.

"…That no bloodline exists between you and her …

we must at least acknowledge that there's a chance—"

Iån held the sword aloft before heaving it with all his might down on the glass, which reverberated without shattering.

Oliå cowered on the other side, turning her gaze towards them for the first time, as if sensing their presence. By pure accident, her eyes fell on the king's, who relented, slowly lowering his sword to his feet. The king buried his face in the crook of his elbow as the weapon slid from his hands, clattering onto the stone floor.

"Bring me Taåg."

The old genie arrived at the top of the tower a moment later. He bowed before the king, who was awaiting his former tutor on the final step, above where the archers had been posted. The wind whistled through the arrow slits. Taåg immediately noticed the dried tears on his godson's cheeks.

Iån started to speak, his voice catching in his throat, and Taåg nodded back at him gently. The genie felt as though he had returned to the time when the young king wouldn't lift a finger without his consent. It had been years since he had been treated with so much respect. Taåg listened to Iån for a long while. When the king spoke of the girl, the old man even let Iån rest his brow on his mud-spattered shoulder.

The king was weeping like a child. Taåg held him in his arms, showing him all his compassion and promising to stay by his side. He would go and speak to the girl to establish what they could expect from her. But the king's despair descended into madness. He moaned and dug his nails into Taåg's clothes.

The genie suddenly felt a cold blade by his ear. Iån had drawn his knife and was pressing it into the old man's temple, right in that thin triangle of flesh through which the skull can be pierced.

"Enter that chamber, Taåg, and do not return with bad news. Do you understand, godfather? Do not be the messenger of my misfortune."

Taåg could hear the king's rasping breath, and he felt the tip of the blade dig deeper into his skin.

"And if the news is that she need not die," added the king, "then tell me that she will love me."

Taåg's voice did not falter.

"I will tell you what is true, Majesty."

"Your life rests on her pale shoulders. As does mine."

Iån kissed old Taåg on the forehead and slowly sheathed his weapon.

Then Iån entered the antechamber, where he had already spent so long looking at the girl through the soldered windowpanes, and pressed his head against the glass.

Taåg followed his master in.

He recognized her immediately.

23

IN THE CHAMBER

Taåg was flung violently onto the glass floor, and the door slammed behind him. His eyes darted around the room as he rubbed his aching body.

Oliå jumped to her feet. Something had changed in her: a flash of the lioness crossed her eyes when she saw him.

"I had forgotten you even existed," he said softly as he looked her over.

She could never forget him. Fifteen years earlier, on his orders, she had blocked the source and brought about the queen's death.

"This time, I'm going to need your help," said Taåg.

He wanted to make Oliå believe that he had been thrown into captivity along with her. The king had agreed to this ruse. Taåg knew that for as long as he was in the glass chamber, he would be without his powers, so he had no recourse to magic spells to persuade her. This was hand-to-hand combat, a duel between the fairy and the old genie. He therefore needed to call on other forms of trickery, which was why they were about to speak like two prisoners in the same cage.

Around them, the game of mirrors created a kaleidoscope, reminding Taåg of his years of confinement, of the times he had banged his head against the glass walls in despair.

"We have to help each other," Taåg said anxiously.

Oliå's defiant expression showed that she was less than willing to do this. If he was going to escape from this place with his life, Taåg would have to find a weakness in her soul.

The genie from the marshlands weighed up the situation. If he were to demonstrate that Oliå was not the king's sister, he would save not just his own life but the fairy's too. He would also regain Iån's trust. On the other hand, if she were to remain alive, she would be a constant threat to him. She knew about the crime he had devised; the crime she had unwittingly carried out herself. She had the power to condemn him.

"Do you know why you are here?"

She assumed it was because she had dried up the lake all those years ago: the young king was avenging his mother's death. But she chose not to answer.

"The king considered killing you straight away, but he hasn't done so yet," said Taåg. "You have a greater chance of being released from here than I do."

Her eyes widened a little. The old man had crouched down on one knee, as if placating a wild beast.

Iån looked on from behind the glass wall, without hearing a word of what was being said. He could see Oliå's face reflected a thousand times over in the mirrors.

Inside the glass chamber, Taåg still spoke in a soft voice, forced to call on charms other than those he normally used.

"The king wants to know if you are a fairy."

He picked up his staff from next to his foot.

"Now, I am well aware that you are." He smiled. "But that response alone will not suffice."

"I don't want to be a fairy any more," Oliå blurted out.

"Why?"

She immediately regretted saying anything, but Taåg seized on her confession.

"In that case, allow the king to love you."

He saw a flicker of curiosity pass over Oliå's eyes. Taåg pressed on, convinced that he had found his solution.

"Only a royal kiss can take away the powers of a fairy. Everyone knows that."

This was no lie. Indeed, it was the oldest of all fairy laws. The idea of this kiss represented Taåg's chance: he would deliver the girl to the king and render her powerless by taking away her magic. All he would have to do then would be to keep her quiet.

"Has nobody ever told you that?"

No, nobody had. Who would have? Who could she have asked? She had learned what it was to be a fairy all by herself.

Oliå seemed to have retreated into herself as she pondered what she'd just heard. So there was a reason for the sudden weakness she had started feeling all those months ago. What bound her to Iliån had begun to change her, and all it would take was a kiss to complete her transformation.

Taåg had no way of knowing her thoughts while she was in this trance-like state.

"You must not talk of what happened before the queen's death. Do you understand?"

She looked at him, troubled. So the king knew nothing of the dried-up lake: that wasn't the reason for her capture.

"Do as I tell you," said Taåg, "and you will be freed

from this prison and from your powers. Then you can speak on my behalf to our king..."

Oliå wore an air of innocence that made her look a few years younger, and Taåg believed that victory was within his grasp.

"Let's make a pact," he proffered. "I want a sign of our agreement. Take my hand."

This was the prearranged signal for those outside the chamber to bring him out.

Oliå looked at the old genie's outstretched hand, while her own was still resting on her wound.

Lower down, at the foot of another of the winter castle's towers, in the armoury, a young man had just pulled on an archer's leather tunic to disguise himself in the throng. Despite being prince of this ancestral castle, and next in line to the throne, it was the first time he had entered its walls.

Iliån knew that Oliå was being held somewhere in this citadel, and he had come to rescue her.

Taåg's dry hand was hovering near the fairy's face.

"Quick, I'm afraid they'll come to take me."

On the surface, it might have looked as if Oliå was still deliberating her decision, but inside she was in no doubt whatsoever. How could she refuse a royal kiss when it represented her chance to be with Iliån? She reached out and touched the old man's hand with her fingertips. The pact was sealed.

The door swung open and two guards entered the glass chamber, grabbing Taåg and dragging him back into the antechamber, where they were joined by the king.

None of them noticed that Oliå had pounced soundlessly behind the door and was now hidden there, breathing quickly. Her powers were almost within reach: she just had to make it through the opening, outside the glass chamber, and they would take effect again.

The chamber door started to close.

The archers didn't move, their eyes trained on the chamber. Slowly the fairy stood up, but they still didn't spring into action. Three armed men and Taåg were blocking her way as the remaining gap narrowed: what did they have to fear, when there was no way through for her?

Yet right there in front of them, as each part of Oliå's body crossed the threshold of the chamber, it regained its magical qualities and evaporated into thin air.

Oliå was vanishing.

The men looked at each other in astonishment,

searching frantically for the captive. Iån had flown into a rage, swiping the air with his sword.

There was nobody.

"She's still here!" Taåg screamed. "Don't move. She has to be here."

He knew that she didn't have the powers to disappear completely. The archers were rooted to the floor, speechless.

Taåg focused his mind, and his eyes immediately darted towards the king's sword. A fly had landed on the scarlet blade.

"There!" cried Taåg.

Before he had taken a step, a blue snake started slithering down Iån's sword, which the king swirled round his head, flinging the serpent across the room; the next instant, everyone heard a sound like a small flag being unfurled. Two wings had just opened, and a bat was racing towards the exit.

Realizing what he had to do, Taåg squatted down on his haunches: a scab-ridden dog suddenly burst from his clothing and tore after Oliå.

Passing through the group of archers guarding the top of the stairway, the bat landed on the ground and swiftly rolled into a ball, emerging in the weasel form of her happiest memories. She ran between the soldiers' legs and hurtled down the steps. The dog was gaining on her, but already he was panting hard, spittle slathering down his yellow coat. He crashed into anyone who tried to stop him, as a cry went up that there was a rabid dog on the loose. Out ahead, the brown-and-white spotted weasel slipped into the castle's labyrinthine corridors.

Down in the lower chambers, the dog lost the scent and started howling in fury: the weasel had disappeared. The hound staggered through the shadows for a long time before collapsing in a heap.

Later, the archers picked up the old genie from the slopping-out area next to the kitchens, and brought him before the king.

Meanwhile, Oliå had come to a halt beneath a bench in a deserted room. She was on the alert, her muzzle to the ground, perfectly poised. She wasn't thinking about her pursuers any more, nor about the mangy dog that had tried to trick her in that glass chamber. All her thoughts were on *him*. She had just felt his presence. He was very near her, somewhere within the castle walls. She knew it. He had come for her.

Up on the ramparts, among the men standing guard in the stormy night, Iliån was hearing rumours that a girl had escaped.

"A girl?"

"They say she's a sorceress."

The soldiers spoke to him as though he was one of their own. They had been sent to check the high bridges that led up to the towers, a perilously exposed part of the fortifications where none of them would dare to venture for fear of falling victim to the fugitive's powers.

Iliån made his way up there, battling against the winds that howled through the black stone crenellations. He had to find her before anyone else did.

But she was the one who spotted him. She was creeping along a thin ledge, keeping perfect balance despite the battering wind. Suddenly she saw a shadow stealing across a bridge that led directly into the tower below her. The sound of the sea would have muffled her pitiful weasel's cries, so she hurled herself into the void before he could disappear from sight.

"Oliå."

Slowly, she got to her feet. She had just expelled the animal from her for the last time. Now she was standing before Iliån, numb with cold.

He took her in his arms and kissed her.

They were found intertwined in the grain store on the

ramparts. The next thing she knew, she was torn from him.

"Who was the person they found with her?" asked the king, ready to strangle the messenger. "Who is he?"

In giving his answer, Taåg was saving his skin: this was his last chance of redemption. He had read Iliån's face as though it were the page of an open book.

"He's your brother, Majesty."

Day was breaking and the young king was standing on the battlements. The breeze was warmer now, and it fanned his desire for revenge.

Oliå had been locked in a simple cell, since all of her powers had deserted her overnight. From now on, nothing of the fairy remained in her. She would just be ever so slightly more lost, more sensitive, more beautiful than any other girl her age. She was wearing the sling shot Iliån had given her, wrapped around her wrist.

Prince Iliån was entrusted to Taåg, who was to execute him in secret by the lightship. But the wicked old genie, afraid of being cursed as a king-slayer, did not kill the second in line to the throne.

So he banished Iliån instead, sending him into an exile from which he would never return. Oliå didn't arrive in time to bring him back. And then she too disappeared. Long after the event, they found a cord hanging from her tower window. She had made it by tying clothes together, before escaping into the night.

In the bleak years that followed, legends abounded as to what had become of her. There was talk of a young girl at the bottom of the sea, or hiding somewhere else to prepare her revenge. The people, oppressed by the king's madness, made her into their secret heroine. That is the way stories are born, when small mysteries meet dark times.

Only Taåg and the keeper of the lightship knew what had really happened in Oliå's final moments in the Kingdoms.

Taåg had arrived on horseback by the beach, where he had found Oliå with the keeper. To save his own skin, the genie had banished her too. She begged him to let her go. And so it was that she had latched onto the spell that had taken Iliån away, grabbing hold of it as though it were the tail of a comet.

But in return she'd had to accept a terrible demand from Taåg, his sole condition for her living in the same world as Iliån: she was not to be seen by her beloved. If, at any point in his exile, the former prince discovered Oliå's presence, she would disappear forever.

And so it was that a fifteen-year-old girl alighted in

our world, amid the chaos of the same storm, on that same evening in September 1936. The midnight bells were sounding from church to church across the Paris rooftops.

Iliån had arrived a few hours before her.

Standing at the Pearls' window, his red blanket clasped around his neck, he was already drinking rainwater from his cupped hands. How he would have loved to know that she was passing along the pavement just below, in her white shift, and trailing her hand against the walls as she gazed up towards him.

PART THREE

LOST FRAGMENTS FROM
THE KINGDOMS

24

BASTILLE DAY BALL

IT HAPPENED TWO YEARS AGO.

I had returned to Paris in the middle of the summer to spend a couple of days doing some library research, leaving my wife and daughter behind in the torpor of the holidays, far from the city. When the time came for me to leave, I went along with their show of feeling sorry for me.

"Come back quickly."

"Have fun, the pair of you."

Both sides played their parts, in the knowledge that happiness is woven of such comings and goings: one train sloping off, another pulling in; headlights appearing at the end of the drive, or the sound of a tooting horn growing fainter in the distance; the hum of the engine as the coach pulls away on a school trip, leaving the parents staring at one another like idiots on the pavement ("Right, what now?") in the knowledge that the children are already singing lustily inside the coach that smells of crisps and new anoraks.

Happiness is a dance where each step brings you closer together or further apart, but you never lose sight of one another. You could even say that it's made from the tears of separations, safe in the knowledge that there will always be reunions.

In my case, I wasn't going very far, or for very long, and if I hadn't yet booked my return ticket for a couple of days' time, it was just to savour the heady sense of freedom.

During the train journey, I had used up several pages of my notebook listing all the research I intended to undertake. I was prepared, with my collection of library cards bulging in my pocket. I was embarking on a long writing project, and needed to visit a number of libraries. All being well, I'd have my answers in two days.

As it turned out, I never set foot inside a single library. They were all shut for three days. Going from closed-door to closed-door, I concluded my tour with a fruitless visit to the Mazarine Library, then I sat down on the steps in front of the Seine to take stock in the afternoon sunlight.

The truth was, I felt more ridiculous than desperate.
I could hardly complain: it was a sunny day, Paris
was overrun with strolling visitors, and the cars had
deserted the city. I caught snatches in every language
from the loudspeakers on the Bateaux-Mouches: the
onboard tourist guides were holding forth about the
Île de la Cité, the Academie Française and a queen who
used to hurl her lovers from the top of a tower.

These snippets of stories, combined with those
figures passing in front of me – the broken heel of
a woman on the cobblestones; the little girl playing
cup-and-ball with her scoop of ice cream; the man
proclaiming "Versailles!" while pointing to the
Louvre, as his beloved, in raptures over so much
culture, took his face in her hands and kissed him –
all this was worth the treasures of a library.

I don't know how long I stayed there, dreaming on
those steps.

Bells had just chimed on the other side of the Seine
when three girls made their way towards me. One of
them enquired whether I spoke any English. I confirmed
that I did, with a modest *"Yeees I dooo"* straight out of
my first English textbook.

This encouraged another of the girls to start gab-
bling so fast I couldn't catch a word she said. But

I carried on nodding, for the sake of appearances. It was only when a long silence followed that I deduced she must have asked me a question.

I stared as she waited for an answer, her blue eyes filled with hope. The other girl, who looked about eighteen, sensed my uncertainty. She uttered one word, which she pronounced clearly, and in a tone of voice that was unmistakably a question. This time, I immediately recognized the word *pompier*. She said it again.

"*Pompier?*"

No doubt about it: she had said the word "fireman" in French.

So I nodded even more energetically, like those little dogs with bobbing heads you see in the backs of cars. Yes, yes, yes, *pompier*, I'd heard her right. Fireman. Indeed. Absolutely. But although we were talking about the same thing, I still didn't have the faintest idea why.

She repeated the word a third time, so insistently that I felt it necessary to defend myself.

"Me *not* fireman," I said, thumping my chest. "Me *not* fireman."

I was worried they might suddenly ask for my help in an emergency operation involving cardiac massage and a long ladder.

They managed not to laugh while I gesticulated wildly. But my alarm was only increased when two of them started performing a little dance on the spot, topped off with that word *pompier* again, pronounced with varying degrees of success.

I blushed, and the third girl discreetly advised them to give up, while smiling at me so pityingly that even I began to feel sorry for myself.

Just as they were about to give up and return to the Pont des Arts, I saw the No. 24 bus pass by, decked out with red, white and blue flags on the front. Everything suddenly became clear. I leapt to my feet.

"*Pompier!*" I shouted. "Fireman!"

They turned around. Now it was my turn to give a little sway of my hip, followed by a tango or waltz step.

Of course: they were trying to find the Firemen's Ball. It was the eve of the Bastille Day celebrations, and they were looking for the Firemen's Ball, which was an old tradition on the 14 of July. We fell into one another's arms. *Pompier!*

I offered to lead them to the nearest fire station.

"*Really?*" one of them asked.

"*What a gentleman!*"

"*Fantastic!*"

The three girls expressed their gratitude by talking the whole way there. They each had a thousand interesting things to say, and all spoke over each other. When one of them did pause, it was to laugh very loudly, perform a little dance and point at me; I pretended to be in on the joke, as one of them slapped me on the back, while the others seemed to play out the scene we'd just experienced. Then they picked up the tangled threads of their conversations again.

For the quarter of an hour it took us to stroll up Rue de Seine, Rue de Buci and a few other streets, I didn't understand a single word, but since they'd decided I was a French gentleman I didn't want to let the side down.

I knew the fire station on Rue Madame because my older brother had celebrated his seventh birthday there. We didn't live far away, and our school was in the same street. My brother had invited his friends to visit the fire station, and I was deemed too little to join them. But three or four is the age at which firemen are gods: I've never forgiven him for denying me that visit.

Thirty-five years later, and in the company of three female students, I arrived in front of the same fire station. It was heaving with people, and we could hear the music coming from inside. This was my moment of revenge on my brother.

My new friends tugged at my arm, begging me to go in with them. They seemed thrilled at having finally tracked down the kind of Frenchman – gallant, helpful and good-humoured – that had proved elusive throughout their trip. That said, there was a moment when I thought one of the girls might have mentioned Monsieur Hulot to her friend, while glancing at me; as if she'd spotted a vague resemblance to the French comic character who inspired Mr Bean. But I'd like to think I misheard.

The firemen's ball filled the area at the back of the fire station, where perhaps a thousand people were dancing. Unfortunately, there wasn't a single fire engine in sight, and the few real firemen on the premises were manning the bar and not even wearing their helmets. I couldn't conceal my disappointment.

My new friends instantly found an army of students who looked just like them. They tried to introduce me against a backdrop of deafening music. Some of them shook my hand respectfully, and I suddenly realized that although I was fulfilling the dream of a four-year-old boy, I was actually thirty-nine, and in their eyes this meant I was at least ninety years their senior.

I slipped away, pushing through the crowd and leaving them to the immortality of youth.

Around me, the swaying of the dance held me captive. I was trapped in a shoal of fish, at the mercy of the wave's ebb and flow. Sometimes, the dancers raised their arms in the air, and I couldn't even see the sky any more. I lifted my arms too, for camouflage. I made the most of the din by joining in the chorus like I was in the shower. The faces were spinning so fast they were a blur. The pace was making me feel dizzy. The ground was shuddering as if a herd of dinosaurs had just surrounded Paris.

Suddenly, in the midst of this throng, I froze. Everything else receded for a few seconds. For some curious reason, my thoughts turned to Joshua Pearl. I'd just had a flashback to running through the woods, aged fourteen, and waking up in Joshua Pearl's home. All the energy drained from my body as I felt myself being swept along by the crowd.

When I came to my senses moments later, the noise was unbearable and there seemed to be fog everywhere. I glanced around to see what might have awakened this memory. I must have looked very dazed, because two firemen rose up out of the mist, grabbed hold of me and dragged me off the dance floor.

I should have been thrilled to see my heroes in action close-up, thrilled at the prospect of telling my family about my visit to the fire station and about taking a dizzy turn and being rescued, but none of this could have been further from my mind. I was thinking of Joshua Pearl, of heavy eiderdowns, and dogs, of the fire, our conversations, the suitcases, the treasure, the roasted starlings, and of that day when he had left me in the grass, close to my bike, having taken my camera and photos off me.

"Do you live far?" asked one of the firemen.

"No."

The truth was, I lived far enough, on the other side of the Seine, but my mother's apartment was near by. It was the apartment where I was born and where I had grown up. Like a small boy, I showed the firemen my keys.

"Would you like us to accompany you?"

"No. I'm feeling better now."

"Take it slowly on your way home."

If he thought I was too old for these kinds of parties; what he didn't realize was that, a few seconds earlier, frozen on the dance floor, I had reverted to being fourteen again.

I felt exhausted as I made my way back to my

mother's apartment block; still, I kept turning around to check whether a fire engine might perhaps be following me. I knew my mother was away for the month of July. After heading up to the third floor, I let myself in and flopped on her sofa.

For twenty-five years, the memory of the house with the suitcases had remained my big secret. A secret that had begun as an obsession: on returning home, after my stay with Pearl, I had pinned up Ordnance Survey maps on the walls in a bid to find the exact location of the house; I had calculated my speed through the forest; I had tried to work out the distance covered on foot from my bicycle to the river. My obsession turned to anger. In my notebooks, I kept lists of Joshua Pearl's collection, or what I could remember of it; I drew maps.

The following summer, I'd spent two more days exploring, my excuse being that I was attending another course. Why did they let me set off again, when I had lost all of the family's photographic equipment the previous year? Parents are sometimes hard to fathom.

I was only allowed to take a disposable camera with me. I scoured the forests for three days without finding the boat, the girl, Pearl's house or my photographs.

Great secrets that go unshared begin to fade a little. Their shapes shift beyond recognition, as the secrets themselves become indistinguishable from dreams. When we try to re-awaken them, they only remind us of our solitude.

As I grew up, I felt those memories dissolving inside me. They hadn't disappeared, but they had become ingrained in who I was. I was involved in theatre, I wrote stories, I made things or fixed them, I read books. Joshua Pearl was part of all of that. I no longer sought him out in other places. I didn't even try to disturb him in the depths of my memory.

But he wasn't far.

That night, he had popped up in the most unlikely place, on the makeshift dance floor of a fire station. Something had made him re-surface, in much the same way as the smell of toast in the morning reminds me of my grandfather, or the smell of oil paints can bring my father back to life for a second.

I slept on the sofa, in the same place where I had collapsed twenty-five years earlier after returning from my stay with Pearl.

The next morning, very early, as I was setting off in search of a café that might be open on Bastille Day,

I found a package covered in white tissue paper outside the door to my mother's apartment. It was waiting for me on the doormat, like a small, tired dog returning home after running away.

25

MEMORIES

It was a square box in polished wood, with finely grooved beading to secure the sliding lid; and two slightly darker circles that receded when I pressed on them. Just holding it was enough to bring back the previous day's dizziness.

The fine craftsmanship was a telltale sign, as was the tissue paper, which I instantly recognized; even though the wrapping had been folded inside out so that at first glance I couldn't see the *Maison Pearl* emblem.

Lifting the lid revealed a first layer containing the camera and the seven films. Each item was held in its own perfectly fitted compartment. The camera didn't seem to have suffered, and it was indeed my father's. I was reminded of his hands at work on it, and of the third eye on his chest when he wore it slung around his neck.

I noticed the ribbons in the corners for lifting the first layer, but I was wary of confectionery boxes that trick you into hoping for two layers of chocolates when there's only one. Not that this was *Maison Pearl*'s style. On the lower layer was the Super 8 camera, together with its two films. Everything was magically made-to-measure. Two leather strips held the cartridges firmly in place, and felt-lined dividers supported the movie camera.

I could feel my heart racing as I stared at the box in front of me on the kitchen table.

Legend had it that a slim volume of Molière's plays – stolen from the family home during the Second World War – had been returned by a German soldier thirty years later, with a note of apology. But was it fair to make the comparison? Pearl hadn't stolen the images from me. If anything, I was the thief. He had simply reclaimed what I had tried to take from him. So why was he returning them to me now?

As a small boy, I used to watch my uncles playing chess, sitting stock still beneath a parasol for hours on end. I always wondered what they were waiting for.

Now, I was like a player contemplating a game of chess, occasionally picking up one of the objects only to put it back down again. Time seemed to stand still around me. I didn't move a muscle as I tried to figure it all out. Ocassionally I would lean over the box to breathe in the smell of the wood, to find a message, a folded note somewhere, an explanation.

Eventually, I put the lid back on the box and stood up.

The key to the cellar was on the tray in the hall.

I headed downstairs, rapping on the caretaker's window on my way down. Behind her, in her office, I could see the Bastille Day parade on the television.

The caretaker had a towel wrapped round her head. When she saw me, she pulled a sorry face to let me know my mother wasn't there. She looked like a saleswoman apologizing for not having the right model in stock.

"Maybe at the end of the month."

She waved her hand breezily, as if to imply the management couldn't commit to a specific delivery date. But when I asked her whether she'd left a package in front of my door, her expression turned very serious. She replied that today was a public holiday – in case I hadn't noticed – that she wouldn't be climbing any stairs, and that in any event there was no post on the 14 of July.

Behind her, the planes in the parade flying across

the screen served as a reminder that I was intruding on a day of national celebration. We heard them shortly afterwards, roaring overhead above the apartment block, ready to bombard me for being so disrespectful. It was time to leave the caretaker to the marching columns of the French Foreign Legion.

I rummaged around in the cellar for quite some time, before emerging with a box full of papers spattered with plaster.

Two hours later I was on the train, trying to keep my voice down while using my phone.

"I'm not coming back tonight. I'm making slower progress than expected."

Through the window, the forests hurtled past at three hundred kilometres an hour.

"I'd better hang up. I'm in the library."

Sensing that the entire train was listening to me, I tried to muffle the last word with my hand.

"Where?" inquired the voice on the other end of the line.

"In the library!"

On cue, a loud announcement from the buffet car came over the tannoy, promoting a range of hot and cold snacks, beverages and light refreshments.

"Are you on the train?"

"Not at all. My neighbour's just fooling about. He wants me to hang up."

I was hunched over my phone, forehead to my knees, but I could tell that my neighbour had heard every word.

"I've got to go, I'll call you back when I've arrived – I mean, when I'm on my way…"

I hung up quickly to avoid tying myself in any more knots. I didn't even know why I was lying.

"Sorry, that was my wife," I told my neighbour.

"Yes, I'd got that. Bravo."

He buried himself in his magazine, and I didn't pay him any further notice. I had enough on my mind already. I was heading west, towards the edge of the forest that had been haunting me since the night before.

I changed trains several times. The last one I took seemed unchanged since the day when I had travelled to the region for the first time. It stopped at ghost stations, just as it had done back then. I even thought I recognized the man who was fast asleep behind me, and the woman struggling with the broken lock on the toilet door.

* * *

Before leaving Paris, I'd taken the maps I had retrieved from the cellar and spread them out on a table. The area that interested me was at the intersection of four different maps. I could remember, years earlier, spending whole nights overlaying the corners so that they gave a clear overview.

But this time around, sitting in my mother's kitchen, I opened the laptop I'd fished out of my bag. In a matter of seconds, I was a bird flying over the region that was reproduced with perfect accuracy on the map. How might things have turned out if I'd possessed this diabolical machine at fourteen?

It took me less than five minutes to understand what had kept me awake at night for all those years. Pearl had gone into hiding in a geographical void, in the gap between four pieces of a jigsaw puzzle. He'd had it all planned out: relying on a loop in the river which didn't feature on any map, and which rendered my overlaying of the maps pointless.

Today, satellites had remedied this mistake. On the screen, I followed the river between the green markings of the forests. I was like a wild duck heading upstream in full flight.

And then the house appeared.

It was a small rectangle, the colour of terracotta.

Zooming in, I could even see the pontoon, which seemed to be disappearing into the sand. I was looking for something else, a trace, a presence, as if Pearl might still be there, waving to me from his island.

When I stepped off the train, my first impulse was to find the spot I had set out from all that time ago. But this proved the worst way to begin my explorations.

I found the back road, but it had grown very wide and busy. I had abandoned my bicycle at the exact same spot, twenty-five years earlier. Now, cars roared past me, and the telephone box had been replaced by a triangular sign alerting drivers to the risk of wild animals crossing the road. I felt an urge to paint a bright red car on the sign, warning the poor stags of the dangers *they* faced in the vicinity.

I set off through the woods. My map was virtually useless under the trees. I wandered blindly, in the belief that I was recapturing those smells, the memories of my flight, the sting of nettles and the stubbornness of brambles snagging my legs.

A few hours later, I was sure I couldn't be far from my goal – if only on the basis of how exhausted I felt. I was expecting to see the river or the outline of the house behind the trees. Just then, a poultry lorry passed by right in front of me, leaving me stunned and surrounded by feathers. I was back at the road.

The sun was setting. I had blisters on every toe and insects in my hair. I needed to find another way of going about this.

Perhaps taking pity on my tragic appearance, a woman pulled up and offered me a lift to the nearest village.

"Are you lost?"

"No. I'm just out for a walk."

"Are you sure you're OK?"

Beside her in the passenger seat, I must have looked as pathetic as a shrivelled old mushroom.

She dropped me off on a stone bridge in front of the church. I noticed a Bastille Day Chinese lantern hanging from the balustrade as I heard the car drive away.

Leaning over the greenish water, I knew at once what my plan was for the following day.

I spent a peaceful night in a hotel called *Le Cheval Blanc*. I'd called home again, and managed to entangle myself further. I don't remember what I said to my family that evening to justify a further postponement to my return: probably something about a hostage crisis in the library, or a train in the Metro being derailed.

By seven the next morning, I was gliding in a boat between the alder and poplar trees. The hull crushed the water-lily pads, but the flowers popped back up again like corks; dragonflies landed on the oars; I had the feeling of returning to a source. Scattered on the banks, the few morning fishermen disappeared eventually. I could see trees leaning over the water and, in their shadows, fish rising to the surface. It was already hot.

It was scarcely ten o'clock when I recognized, to my left, the detour that didn't feature on any map. The river divided in two. So I followed the loop, occasionally leaving my oars in the water to take a close look at the map from the cellar. On that paper faded like parchment, the rectangle representing the house was still there.

And then, after another bend in the river, I saw the tiled roof.

I had done the sums a hundred times: how many years had elapsed, how long a man might live... I knew that what I was hoping for didn't make any sense. But was there anything sensible about this story? As I approached the house, I was convinced I would see Pearl and his old dogs coming to meet me.

The pontoon was covered in sand. I ran my boat

aground and stepped onto the bank. The door hadn't swung open. The walls and roof were being eaten by vegetation. I took a few steps in the long grass.

"Monsieur Pearl?"

I called out faintly enough for there to be a chance that he might not have heard me; a chance that this could be the reason for him not appearing. It was a bright sunny day, after all, and he'd probably stayed inside in the shade. Pearl would be over eighty by now. He had every right not to come to meet me. He would be asleep in his lumpy old toad of an armchair.

"Can I come in?"

When I pushed the door open, it fell straight down like a drawbridge.

Coming from the midday glare, my eyes took a while to adjust to the interior of the house. I edged forwards along the door, which was now lying in the dust. The house must have been deserted for some years. There was no sign of anyone living there. The bed, the dresser, the stone sink – they had all disappeared. And the great wall that had so enchanted me? Those hundreds of piled-up suitcases? Where were they? What traveller could set off with so much luggage? An Arabian prince leading his caravan of camels?

The evidence suggested that I'd dreamt it all up,

that I'd furnished this place with my imagination.

Which was why I latched onto the old circular saw that had been left in a corner. It was exactly as I remembered it, with its belt and motor. There used to be a bicycle propped up against it. I suddenly found myself wondering how a saw had found its way into Joshua Pearl's house, and why I had never been surprised by its presence. Is it normal to have an enormous saw next to a bed? Or a bicycle? Even those memories I thought I was rediscovering seemed to be faltering.

I moved deeper into the gloom, searching for anything I might recognize: a forgotten suitcase or the dogs' drinking bowl. But all I found were the ruins of a gutted barn on the banks of a river. I leant against a beam and stared at the light filtering in through the windows.

I had been inside here before, I was sure of that. I remembered the fire and the kettle, the smell of the dogs returning from their swim and the stormy grey of Pearl's eyes. I didn't need to find any traces of him. I wanted to find out where he'd gone, and why I'd been sent that box. What was I meant to do?

Stepping back across the threshold, I put my hand up to sheild me from the glare of the sun. Then, as I flanked the wall of the house, between the water and the pear trees, my foot tripped on something.

There, covered in wild grasses, was a mound of earth, rectangular-shaped. I knelt down, with both knees on the ground, and brushed aside the reeds and butterflies.

It was a grave.

26

OLD BEFORE HIS TIME

Nobody who lived in Paris during the post-war years could fail to remember *Maison Pearl*.

The tiny size of the confectionery shop belied its extraordinary success. Throughout the neighbourhood, people would speak of the Jewish couple, murdered in the war, whose only son had taken on the business in 1945 at the age of twenty-five. On his return, the young Joshua Pearl's first job in the shop had been to chase out the brigands; they had used it as a secret base for their thriving black-market operations during the last years of the war. Behind the lowered iron shutter, they had stockpiled mountains of cured meat and sugar, all with the tacit blessing of the police, who had themselves been bribed with sherry and wine from Spain.

The Pearl boy spent the first year restoring the

ransacked shop. He only had one photograph showing how the window looked before, and he set to work, single-handedly repairing the woodwork, brass and mirrors. He re-established relations with suppliers, and brought up old vats and marshmallow moulds from the cellar. He even managed to unearth the shop's emblem, with its pearl-studded crown.

Maison Pearl reopened its doors in the autumn of 1946. It was an immediate success, despite the shortages that marked those years. French confectionery had always enjoyed a fine reputation, dating back to the end of the previous century, but the decade after the war was etched into the memory of many a sweet-toothed Parisian as the "marshmallow years".

Pearl worked day and night, entirely on his own, without even an assistant to help in the kitchen. He made, sold and delivered marshmallows by the thousand. His working day never ended: he even slept under the counter in the shop instead of using the apartment up on the first floor, which was kept sealed off behind its curtains.

The modest glory of *Maison Pearl* did not come without jealousy. The rumours began appearing in the very first year, but thankfully they were swept aside swiftly enough. When the war was over, there was a lot of talk about swindlers passing themselves off as the descendants of dead or missing families. Neighbouring shopkeepers started saying that the Pearls' son had died of Spanish flu ten years earlier, and that the "Pearl" who'd inherited the business was just another impostor fleecing the dead and turning a profit out of tragedy.

These suspicions threatened to become serious, until one morning a small glass display case appeared next to the cash register. It looked like a miniature cabinet of curiosities, and inside it were half a dozen war decorations, military crosses and Resistance medals, as well as army enlistment records in the name of Joshua Pearl, photographs of him in his Spahi uniform, and letters bearing the signature of a colonel and a politician.

Until that moment, Pearl had never mentioned his military achievements. There was even a theory that he'd spent time in America, what with that strange, unplaceable accent of his. The display was there for barely a week, before disappearing along with the rumour. Pearl was a hero, and this did nothing to help the case of his detractors. Faced with the ever increasing popularity of *Maison Pearl*, they needed to turn their scorn elsewhere, and so started to show an interest in the character and lifestyle of the young man himself.

In this department, there was plenty to gossip about. Joshua Pearl was young, charming and bright-eyed. He had a pleasant manner with customers, visitors and suppliers alike, not to mention the people he met in the street, but there was no escaping the fact that in other ways his behaviour was more than a little odd. By turn, people said he was misanthropic, curmudgeonly, greedy, shifty, antisocial or hypocritical. The girls who had courted him before the war had long since married, though beautiful Suzanne, the plasterer's daughter, who bore him no grudge, still came to buy heaps of marshmallows every Thursday with her three sons, just so she could see him.

The neighbours' gossip had absolutely no effect on business at *Maison Pearl*. People came for the marshmallows that were so alluring in their white tissue paper, or for the charismatic confectioner, or for the aroma of toasted almonds rising up between the floorboards, or for the air so thick it enveloped the customers as they walked in. No amount of jealousy could ever have destroyed that.

The stand-off reached new heights in the second year, when Pearl made the decision to close for three days a week: from now on, the shop would only be open from Tuesday to Friday, eight o'clock to eight o'clock.

The local shopkeepers took this as an affront. They claimed that it had all gone to Pearl's head, that he was showing contempt for his customers, and that he was acting like some kind of film star: haughty, soft in the head, spoilt, smug, selfish, aloof, lazy... No one dared admit that when *Maison Pearl* was closed, the neighbourhood became a wasteland, and that this was the sole reason for their disdain. And so the questions returned: what did he do with all his money? Where did he go when he shut up shop? Did he have girl-friends dotted around the country? Had he bought himself a villa somewhere? The poultry seller on Rue Dupuis told everyone that Pearl was mean and old before his time, and that he was thinking of retire-ment before he'd even turned thirty. He said he saw Pearl setting off every Friday evening with his silly old hat and suitcase.

"If it were my son, I'd feel ashamed," he liked to say, shaking his head. He'd then proceed to look proudly at his own son, who was scrawny as a chicken claw and could barely pluck a bird – while the handsome Pearl did the work of ten men, with a queue of customers stretching all the way back to the square.

"Think of his poor parents!" the poultry seller said. But somewhere up in the confectioners' paradise, Jacques and Esther Pearl must have been bursting with pride.

"You can see it in his eyes," he continued. "I'm telling you: he's mean and old before his time."

When Joshua Pearl went past the poultry seller's with his small suitcase every Friday, he was in fact heading to Gare de l'Est, Gare du Nord or the airport at Le Bourget. He left in the night for Rotterdam or Prague, or else to take the Orient Express and hop out before the Turkish border. He boarded ships at Cherbourg to sail to remote ports in Ireland. He negotiated the canals of Amsterdam in the pitch black, and had meetings at the docks in Gdansk or among the stalls in the market town of Paradas, Andalusia.

If Joshua Pearl chose not to raise the iron shutters outside his shop, it was because he was slipping behind the iron curtain that divided Europe in those days. He went on to defy the wall in Berlin and sneak his suitcases through the barbed-wire fences lining the borders. And if he wasn't up to his elbows in marsh-mallows at 5 a.m. on a Tuesday, it wasn't because he was watering his chrysanthemums at some villa on the banks of the Marne, but because he'd made the journey to Kharkiv or Naples; or because a charlatan was trying to lose him in the streets of Casablanca; or because he was trapped in a snowstorm; or some fraudulent street vendor was making a play for his gold.

In reality, this eligible young bachelor – accused of being old before his time, despite his thirty years, and labelled as avaricious, narrow-minded, idle – sacrificed his days and nights and everything he had earned, because he was consumed with a mad love for a fairy. He never shied away from danger, leaving untold fortunes in the hands of smugglers in order to build up his collection: a more unlikely and ethereal treasure trove of objects than any crazy collector had ever gathered.

As soon as *Maison Pearl* reopened in the autumn of 1946, Joshua started seeking out the doctor from Alsace who had helped him during his time as a prisoner in the stalag. And it wasn't just because he wanted proof of good conduct, to counter the allegations that he wasn't Joshua Pearl – no, he had other plans.

The doctor from the prison camp was very much alive. The two men met in Marseille, where the doctor was about to board a ship for Egypt.

The sun was shining, and they sat on some steps in a small square. Children were playing soldiers all around them.

"I didn't think you'd survived," the doctor smiled.

Pearl shrugged. The memory was still painful.

"Our friend Brahim died," the doctor added, needlessly.

Pearl nodded.

"Kozowski had planned it all along. It never pays to blackmail the devil."

As they watched the children running in the autumn sunshine, the two men reminisced about the morgue that had been the camp infirmary. Somehow all that horror had existed in the same world as this.

"You're leaving," Pearl said, pointing to the doctor's bag.

"Yes. And I'm never coming back. There's an archaeological dig in a valley in Egypt, and I'm going to be their doctor. After that I'll find other tombs to explore, until eventually I reach my own…"

The doctor handed Joshua an envelope.

"Here's the letter you asked for. I say lots of nice things about you."

"It's not for me…"

"I know. Nowadays, they need written proof for

everything, even our nightmares."

Pearl thought of Captain Alexandre's words as he took the letter: *They must have tokens of proof.*

"I wanted to ask you something else," Pearl said.

"Go on."

"Where's Kozo?"

The doctor tilted his face towards the sun a little.

"I cured him, I'm sad to say. I cured him," he admitted, laughing awkwardly. "I promise I didn't do it on purpose."

Pearl didn't flinch.

"Where is he?"

The doctor stopped laughing and looked at Pearl. He could see that the boy wasn't just out for vengeance.

"Still after that mermaid's scale?"

Pearl didn't respond.

"Kozo took it off Brahim. I was there when they brought back the body. I also found out that Kozo had stolen it, before the war, from a Portuguese shoemaker in Cracow."

"Where's Kozowski now?"

"It was the Soviets who liberated the camp. Kozo switched sides straight away. He became their friend and was made interpreter to the general staff."

The doctor got to his feet. It was time for him to leave.

"But don't give up hope. I've already told you: I know about these things. I've been chasing them my whole life... And as you can see, I'm still chasing them."

There was a blast of a ship's horn, and they shook hands.

"Be careful. Mysteries have a habit of slipping through one's fingers."

As he let go of Pearl's hand, he saw the leather cord around his wrist, and hastily lifted the sleeve to reveal the rolled-up slingshot.

"Where did you find this?" the doctor asked.

"It's mine. It comes from the place I call home."

The doctor gazed at the object, as if transfixed by it. Pushing up his glasses, he released Joshua's hand and looked him in the eye, as though he'd known the truth all along.

Over the children's screaming, they heard the boat let out another blast.

The doctor nodded knowingly.

"Kozo's in Moscow," he said, taking a step backwards, his bag slung over his shoulder.

As he went, a child aimed two fingers at him, like a pistol, and fired. The doctor pretended to die, convulsing on the ground. Then he got to his feet, picked up his glasses and went on his way, casting a final backwards glance at Pearl.

27

THE COLLECTION

Who can say how Joshua Pearl made it to Moscow in January 1947? All that matters is that this expedition served as a blueprint for the many others he would make in the following years: a fleeting visit where nobody suspected a thing. Just as you avoid burning your hand when running it through a flame, so Pearl realized that by disappearing as quickly as he arrived, he could confront even the most the merciless of enemies.

Burglars of the more gifted variety know that a successful operation can't be a three-step waltz: arrive, steal, leave. There must only be two phases: arrive, leave. The stealing has to happen – as if by magic – somewhere between the two.

And so it was that Bartosz Kozowski found himself dangling from the ceiling of his office in the Kremlin. He hadn't noticed anyone come in. The mistake he made was to wear a tie as well as the silver cord with the mermaid's scale. A hand came from behind his shoulder and grabbed his tie, hauling him up to the ceiling light above his desk, where he remained for a few seconds with his feet kicking in the air.

The shoddy light fitting was Kozo's salvation. He fell, smashing all his teeth on the edge of his desk. Only then did he discover that his mermaid's scale had disappeared.

Two days later in Paris, Pearl opened the shop five minutes later than usual.

Every time after that (or almost every time) he did his best to refrain from violence or force. After the first expedition, he also made sure that he always settled his debts: the mermaid's scale didn't belong to him, therefore he had to pay for it.

So one month later, he went to Cracow, where he had no trouble finding the city's only Portuguese shoemaker: there weren't many of them in Poland in those days.

It was snowing in the streets. Before entering the shop, Pearl had taken off one of his shoes and struck the sole against the ice hanging from the gutter, causing the heel to fly off.

The old shoemaker, who spoke a little French,

didn't enquire as to what had brought Pearl to Poland – accustomed as he was to being asked the same question himself.

"Shall I mend it straight away?"

"If you don't mind. It's snowing out there, and I don't have anything else to walk in."

"Wait for me here."

The shoemaker slipped his leather apron over his neck and disappeared into the adjacent room, where the sound of hammering started up from his workbench. Pearl slipped behind the counter and began rummaging through compartments that were stuffed with leather, soles and heaps of strange accessories. Kozo's scale had once belonged to this man, so maybe he possessed other treasures too.

With the sound of filing now audible from the workshop, Pearl stooped to pull out a box from the lowermost shelf. It had been nailed shut, but he managed to prise it half open, thrusting both his hands inside.

"Don't move."

Pearl turned round.

"I said don't move."

The shoemaker was wielding a shotgun with barrels wide enough for a man's arm to fit through.

"Hands up."

Pearl removed his hands from the box. They were black with boot polish. Turning his head slowly, he saw that the old man was shaking.

"What are you looking for?"

Pearl could tell that the shoemaker was ready to fire.

"Did he send you again?" he asked.

"I don't understand," Pearl said.

"I told them I don't have anything else. Your lot have already come here twice."

"Are you talking about Kozowski's men?"

The shoemaker was still shaking.

"I punished him," said Pearl. "Kozowski will never come back."

"So what are you doing here?"

"I would like to make good his debts."

This surprising tactic could have triggered a violent reaction.

"Look in my pocket," said Pearl. "There's a white package."

The old man looked out of his depth, as he lowered his weapon.

"Give me the coat," he said.

The snow had melted on Pearl's shoulders. Very slowly he shrugged off the heavy coat, which the shoe-maker took in one hand, with the shotgun weighing heavily on his other arm. He started searching in the pocket.

"Put your weapon down," Pearl said. "It's not loaded."

"How would you know?"

"It's a customer's gun. They brought it in for you to mend the leather strap. Put it down. I want to talk to you."

Sure enough, only half of the embroidered leather strap that was hanging below the shoemaker's arm had been re-stitched. Trembling more than ever, he slowly lowered the gun and laid it on the counter.

Pearl watched as the man removed the white *Maison Pearl* package. He opened it a fraction before rushing to double-bolt the shop's door. Then he returned to count the notes.

"I'm paying on Kozo's behalf," Joshua explained. "I'm the one who rescued the mermaid's scale he stole from you."

The old shoemaker wiped his forehead with his sleeve: the bundle of notes wrapped in this paper was roughly equivalent to the value of his shop.

"Where did you find the mermaid's scale?" asked Pearl, walking over to the shop window to glance down the street.

"The story goes back a long way. A German man wanted to pay for an overcoat and a pair of boots. He'd lost everything in the first war. The mermaid's scale was all he had left. He ended up wandering across Europe, and drinking heavily."

"Do you remember his name?"

"No. Later on, a man tried to buy it off me. He was from Lisbon, like me. A coffee merchant. His name was Caldeira. I think he was the one who told Kozowski I had the scale."

Pearl realized that there was nothing more for him here, and put on his coat.

"What you gave me – it's too much money," said the man. "I got the scale thirty years ago for the price of a pair of boots."

"So why not throw in my repair for free?"

As the man went to fetch the shoe from the workshop, Pearl thought of one more thing.

"You said the German bought a pair of boots and a coat?"

"Yes."

"He paid for the boots with the mermaid's scale…"

"Yes."

"What about the coat?"

The old man smiled. First he helped Pearl put on

his shoe, before carefully lacing it for him. Then he stood up and tore off a square of leather that had been stitched onto the front of his shoemaker's apron, and put it in front of Pearl.

"He bought the coat with this."

It was a piece of tanned hide with a copper-threaded trim. Pearl paused a moment before picking it up. Instantly he felt the object's peculiar vibration. The talent that would turn him into such a fearsome relic-hunter was making itself known even now. Nobody could deceive him when it came to identifying tokens of proof from the Kingdoms. This wasn't so much skill as an intimate memory of things. After all, who can fail to recall the scent of lilac from their childhood, or the feeling of sand sticking to their body when rolling on the beach after swimming?

"Do you know what it is?" the shoemaker asked.

Pearl nodded slowly. It came from an ogre's seven-league boot, and it was in immaculate condition.

"I'm giving this to you," said the shoemaker, pulling off his apron solemnly. "You're an honest man. As for me, I'm going to close down the shop and live out the rest of my days in my homeland."

Pearl held the piece of leather against him. His collection was beginning to grow.

"Remind me, what was the name of the coffee merchant you mentioned?"

"Caldeira."

They shook hands, and the shoemaker turned out the lights.

Pearl returned to Paris and opened the shop at eight o'clock on Shrove Tuesday morning. He served no fewer than two hundred customers that day. Forty-eight hours before, he had given away all the money he had earned since opening the shop: he was going to have to work hard to finance this mad quest.

Inside the small suitcase that he'd hidden between the sacks of sugar lay a mermaid's scale and part of a seven-league boot wrapped in *Maison Pearl* tissue paper. Together with the slingshot that never left his wrist, these were the first jewels of Joshua Pearl's collection; the first pebbles marking the way home for Iliån. It was by gathering these tokens of proof that he would undo Taåg's spell. Gradually, over time, other treasures and other suitcases came to join them.

In Lisbon, Pearl found Vasco Caldeira. The coffee and cocoa dealer had retired ten years earlier and lived in a small house by the sea. Pearl spoke to him of the shoemaker from Cracow, and the old man admitted to having met him, even though Caldeira himself had never been a collector.

"I travelled, and I met a lot of people over the years as I loaded ship after ship with bags of coffee. But deep down, all I wanted was to be a pirate. So I started seeking out contraband."

Caldeira went to fetch some paper with a *Portuguese Spice Company* header.

"You're young," he said, sitting down in front of a candle. "What's your interest in all this? You'd be better off falling in love."

"Perhaps," Pearl replied.

In the course of an hour, Caldeira scribbled away on the paper, drawing a map for Joshua Pearl that detailed all manner of information about what he referred to as "contraband".

He gave the names of merchants and the locations of prime areas, such as souks, ports and bazaars. He spoke of the violence of the trafficking routes and networks; of the rivalries. His nib scratched the paper, tracing arrows and weaving links between the continents. Pearl listened attentively to the details of the operations, the rates and the tricks of the trade.

When Vasco Caldeira had rolled up the sheet of

paper and set it alight in the candle flame, he offered a final word of advice.

"Never keep too many of them with you. It always ended badly when people got greedy and wanted too much. Let the objects go."

He wasn't entirely sure how to explain the danger, simply repeating that for collectors who went too far, it ended badly. Very badly.

The paper was still burning on the table.

"Blood and ruin," he kept saying, pointing out at the ocean. "Blood and ruin. That's why I never kept anything. Look at me. I'm doing alright here, aren't I?"

Pearl didn't follow this advice. He sold the furniture from the apartment on the first floor and started stockpiling his treasure there. Ten years later, the suitcases were approaching the sitting room ceiling. In Joshua's old bedroom, it wasn't even possible to open the window. The hoard spilled into the hallway, and Madame Pearl's abandoned kitchen soon looked like a left-luggage office.

Maison Pearl became a small outpost of the Kingdoms; an enclave of the story world. Among Pearl's treasures was a stained-glass window cut into the shape of dragons' claws, a petticoat so worn it had become transparent, and the pip of a famous apple that had been set in amber to prevent it from poisoning anyone. In a particularly emotional purchase, he had even bought a scrap of his own crib that had washed up on the seashore and been passed from hand-to-hand for decades.

One night when Joshua was away from Paris, burglars tried to rob *Maison Pearl*; but they didn't find a single coin in the shop. All the money from the cash register had been spent by Joshua on a mule that was now laden with cases: he was making his way across the mountains by the Italian border. After finding the key to the apartment on the shop counter, the burglars headed upstairs, but they weren't able to push the door open, and eventually they gave up.

When Joshua came home, he discovered the key lying on the stairway carpet. The door was blocked, but he managed to climb up the wall and enter the apartment by breaking a windowpane.

He parted the curtains and saw that all the suitcases had been pushed up against the door, making it impossible to open.

How had his rescuer escaped? For someone had clearly moved two or three hundred suitcases across the room to save the collection. This didn't surprise

Joshua. He had become aware of such fortuitous interventions over the years. But not even this special protection would be enough to save *Maison Pearl* from ruin.

28

BLOOD AND RUIN

The first sign came in the middle of summer in 1959.

Joshua Pearl was in the shop, listening to the sounds of the city. It was in rare moments like this that he was able to imagine not leaving, choosing our world instead, forgetting Oliå. That time of the afternoon, between two and three o'clock, made him perilously fond of his exile.

When he switched off the electric light, the sun would reflect off the wall across the street, setting the brass fittings ablaze. In days gone by, Jacques Pearl called this the "hallowed hour". The coolness from the basement would creep up the iron stairs; not a sound, apart from the occasional word escaping from a window, or a muffled laugh, or birds chirruping on a balcony. Sometimes, though not often at this hour, a customer might push open the door. Pearl would smile at the visitor and return to his dreamlike state.

It could be a young woman, saying something along the lines of, "I left the children asleep upstairs. I know I shouldn't, but I'm feeling peckish."

Pearl would make a broad gesture with his arms as if to say, *Please don't apologize, help yourself.*

She would let her gaze linger on the marshmallows behind the glass, and Pearl would leave her to it.

For once, he wouldn't be thinking about the suit- cases weighing heavily on the wooden floor above his head. He'd watch the woman in front of him who lived in the same world as he did, this world he had found a little drab at first, but which he had now grown fond of. He had become accustomed to its bland nature, its little faults, its dullness; he had even started to see magic in it.

The customer might click her tongue softly to make up for her hesitation, holding her hand to her mouth perhaps, or chewing her lip as she leant forward for a better view.

"They're all so tempting…"

Pearl would smile again and make the same calm and accommodating gesture as before.

He'd reflect on how the two of them were the same age, around thirty-eight or thirty-nine, and he'd wonder for a moment whether he shouldn't just immerse himself in the imperfections of this world, instead of constantly coming up against a glass wall; why not settle down and have children that he too could leave sleeping while he popped out to the shops?

Finally the lady would swoop on the vanilla marshmallow, and he'd prepare the large sheets of tissue paper. At the last minute, she would take a second marshmallow for her husband.

"The same one, yes, the white one."

Two translucent strips of marshmallow would be laid on the white paper, their flecks of vanilla visible on the inside. She would pay and then leave. Silence would return. But it wouldn't last for long, since in a few minutes another customer would come in. And Iliån would think of Oliå again.

It happened in this hallowed hour at the start of the afternoon.

A woman entered the shop carrying a large suitcase. Pearl immediately recognized her as one of the contraband smugglers he'd bought several objects from. But he had never given his name or address to any of his contacts.

Pearl looked at her coldly, as she examined the shop.

She was twenty-five years old, went by the name of Carmen and had a reputation for being a hard-nosed haggler.

"I wasn't sure how to find you," she explained. "Last time, though, I saw *Maison Pearl* on the tissue paper when you were wrapping up the package. So here I am."

Both of them knew that they were breaching the usual code of practice. She put her suitcase down on the floor.

"I think this might be of interest to you," she said.

"There are rules," Pearl replied.

"This one has a peculiar story behind it."

"That doesn't change anything."

"I read that a man had been fished out of a canal in Bruges after a masked ball. Drowned. There was a photograph of his costume in the newspaper. The police were unable to identify him."

Pearl didn't trust this woman. He could tell that there was no glimmer of the story world in her: that glint he was always glad to notice in the other smugglers he worked with, even the most sinister ones.

There were perhaps no more than twenty of them in the world. Some were wanted by every police force on every continent. Their number included dangerous

THE BOOK OF PEARL

lunatics and enlightened beings alike, but all of them shared a single goal: to draw closer to a mystery. Carmen, for her part, was only there for business, nothing more. She would have smuggled cream cheese if there was enough money to be made from it.

"I picked up the clothes from the morgue. No one claimed the body."

Pearl ushered her and her suitcase into the backroom. She continued to glance around as though expecting to discover, framed and up on the wall, the treasures he had previously bought from her at such expense.

Setting the case down on the draining board next to the sink, Pearl proceeded to open it. There under a black cloth was a leather tunic, some gaiters and a broken bow: all the equipment of the archers from the Kingdoms.

He snapped the suitcase shut as if he'd just seen a poisoned dart heading his way. Carmen was looking intently at his face, trying to gauge his reaction.

"I won't buy it."

Pearl uttered these words without betraying his fear, but he was well aware that the archer would not have entered this world without good reason.

"Go away, please."

If the archer had died, others would come in search of Pearl – and Carmen might already have been spotted.

"Leave me be," he murmured. "I'm not buying anything else."

She sighed and sat down on a chair.

"I've travelled far; they told me you'd take all of it. I'm disappointed."

"They lied to you. I've stopped. I make marsh-mallows now."

"Shame," she said.

She made a show of settling in for the long haul, adopting a defiant expression as she sat back in her chair and loosened her collar. Realizing the danger she represented, Pearl took a wad of notes from a drawer and placed them in front of her; she started counting them. It was four o'clock, and the first customers of the afternoon could be heard entering the shop. Children whispered in front of the marshmallows as they waited.

When she'd finished counting, Carmen looked as if she might be about to push her luck, but the stormy grey of Pearl's eyes made her think twice.

"Never come back here again," he said.

She stood up without even glancing at the suitcase, which she left on the draining board, and walked straight into the shop. Suzanne and her children, togther with three others customers saw her appear behind the counter brandishing the wad of notes. Pearl looked very pale, and Suzanne went bright red. She watched Carmen step into the street and wave faintly at Pearl through the window.

He didn't wave back. He had a premonition that this was the end.

For a month after that, Pearl stopped travelling. He didn't have the strength to get rid of Carmen's suitcase. At night, when the shop was closed, he would stay inside. He'd bought dozens of maps of France, and used to pore over them, making notes in every square of the grid. He was already planning his escape.

But one day in September, a temptation came along that he couldn't resist. He'd heard that an object, something that had eluded him several times in the past, would be on sale at a cattle market just outside Paris. It was a thimble made of gold alloy, with, engraved around the outside, a spiral of letters too small to read but said to tell the story that had made the thimble famous.

One Sunday, at four o'clock in the morning, Pearl arrived at the marketplace. The hall was filled with the sound of lowing. Cattle dealers were busy presenting their beasts that had been herded between various barriers. In a corner, a few figures were elbowing their way towards a short man who had cleared a tiny island in the sea of livestock.

The dealer, a Spaniard, greeted Pearl with a nod but didn't look him in the eye. As he brushed down the rump of one of his beasts, he explained through gritted teeth that he was waiting for two buyers before starting the sale; he would give them another five minutes. Pearl immediately stepped away.

But the latecomers never arrived.

At the appointed time, the dealer nonetheless erected a trestle table, and half a dozen people converged around it as though he were about to perform a three-card trick. Pearl had spotted all of them. They came from at least three continents. The Spaniard had displayed the thimble in its red box. Meetings like this never lasted more than two or three minutes. Just as the dealer was about to announce a price, a man appeared in their midst with sweat pouring off his face. The cattle pressed them in from all sides.

"*Falta Carmen?*" the dealer asked, recognizing the man immediately and wondering why he was alone. He had been supposed to arrive with Carmen but, for now, he could barely speak.

"*Se murió Carmen*," the man gasped.

In the time it took to say "Carmen's dead", five of the buyers had already evaporated into the hall.

"Dead?" Pearl asked, drawing closer.

"During the night. She was with me on the train," said the man, pulling a bloodstained arrow from his jacket.

Pearl turned on his heel and sprinted through the mass of animals. Outside in the darkness, he could just distinguish the farmers' vehicles parked in the yard. He noticed a small Citroën cattle truck, which seemed to be the most manageable of all the enormous lorries before him. Pearl climbed in, found the key under the seat, and started the engine. He hadn't driven since his years serving with the *maquis* in Provence. He checked his rear-view mirror, but no one was following him.

At quarter to five in the morning, Pearl re-entered Paris by the Porte d'Orléans. He feared the worst: Carmen knew too much about him. Right from the start, he suspected they would target the woman who had shown too much interest in the corpse in Bruges. She was bound to have said anything to try to save her own skin.

He parked the cattle truck fifty metres from the shop. The morning light had yet to reach the foot of the buildings, and the street was deserted. How could it be that his enemies had still not arrived?

Pearl walked into the shop. No one. He strained his ears for the sound of footsteps above him.

In the space of two hours, he emptied the place. Having moved the truck to below the apartment, he proceeded to throw the suitcases from the window into the back. Eventually he started up the engine and disappeared, unaware that at that very moment, three shadows were picking their way past the chimneys and gutters from the direction of Rue du Faubourg du Temple; three archers leaping noiselessly across the rooftops.

The following day, the police found the shop completely ransacked. The mirrors had been shattered and the display cabinets gutted. Sugar and glass crunched beneath their boots. Upstairs in the apartment, every block of the parquet floor had been ripped out. Not a single piece of furniture was left in any of the rooms.

The neighbours, who insisted they hadn't heard a thing, told the police that none of this came as a surprise: they had never really kept company with the man in question. As if to prove their point, they mentioned that he received women in the backroom of his shop; women who emerged waving banknotes in their hands. The police officers listened to these testimonies as the debris was cleared. There was one girl who ventured inside and wandered around the ruins, but everyone else looked in from the street.

A long way off to the west, a cattle truck was driving down small country lanes bordered by black-berry hedges.

29

THE LIFE OF OLIÅ

At least she would grow old like him: that's what she
had wanted to believe.

She could only look at him, while he would never be
able to see her; yet they would grow old together, and
one day they would die together in the same world.
That was her consolation. But after a few years, whenever she caught her reflection in a mirror, she realized
that even this comfort had been denied her.

Taåg had lied. She had renounced her fairy powers,
yet he had secretly restored her eternal youth, as a
way of keeping her in check. In doing so, Taåg hoped
his grave error towards the king might be reversible.
Although he had sent Oliå far away to save his own
skin, he had made it possible for her to be recalled
one day, unchanged from the morning of her fifteenth
birthday.

Her first months in our world were the most painful. On arriving in Paris, she moved into a building on the opposite bank of the Seine, for fear of crossing paths with Iliån. In the evenings, she looked after an old lady, a former Latin teacher who gave her a room and taught her French. She found a job in the haberdashery section of one of the city's famous department stores by telling them that she was older than she really was. In truth, her beauty was an instant substitute for any application form or identity papers – and this was despite all her best efforts to make herself ugly. Back in those days, around 1937, she wore second-hand clothes she found at a charity stall run by nuns. Up in her bedroom, she'd taken a pair of kitchen scissors to her head, resulting in a hairstyle so terrible it should have been illegal. But two weeks later all her fellow shop assistants at *Bon Marché* had adopted the same look.

Oliå took the name Solange. On occasion, she would venture close to *Maison Pearl*, but she never went in, choosing instead to slip surreptitiously past the shop window. Each time she glimpsed him inside, her heart would skip a beat; a mixture of fear and pure elation. She would run off and seek refuge in a café, where she'd ask for a glass of water and huddle at the end of the counter to catch her breath.

"You seem upset, mademoiselle," the waiter would say, and she would feel relieved that someone had spoken to her: at least it meant she was still there, that she hadn't dissolved into thin air.

"I feel better, the water helped, thank you."

There were times when someone would walk into the café with a marshmallow from *Maison Pearl*. One day a lady even offered her a taste, which she gladly accepted. It was wonderful. She wiped away her tears as they mingled with the icing sugar on her lips. She didn't have the courage to ask whether a young man had wrapped up the marshmallow.

"You ought to go along there yourself, it's just next door."

"I'm not hungry enough today. But yes, I'm sure I will go one day. May I keep the wrapping paper?"

Oliå also roamed the neighbourhood in the evenings, when she was able to hide in the shadows. She would stare at the lights in the shop, and watch Madame Pearl pass by the apartment window upstairs. One night, she saw Iliån walking along the pavement with a girl who was laughing. She wanted to hurl herself into Iliån's arms so that she could disappear forever.

She quit her job abruptly a few days before Christmas in 1938. The department store had been a hive of activity that morning, with shop assistants flitting between the different sections.

"Fourth floor for flannel offcuts."

As the haberdashery customers descended on the ribbons and samples, Oliå was as busy as a worker bee.

"Mademoiselle, please look after this lady who would like some fancy braid."

She rushed around the centre of this battlefield, tidying the trouser buttons in the trouser button drawer, and the brace clips in the brace clip box. When at around eleven o'clock she was asked to take some bobbins up to the women's clothing department on the top floor, she leapt at the chance of a moment's escape.

"Now?" she asked.

"If you would be so kind, Mademoiselle Solange."

She passed the lace counter and took one of the two criss-cross stairways that rose up beneath the dome. With her hand gripping the rail, she gazed upwards so as not to miss any of the marvellous colours filtering through the stained-glass panels above. When she looked down, there he was, almost level with her on the opposite stairway, headed for the ground floor.

He hadn't seen her. She turned and clasped the bag of bobbins, but on reaching the top, she couldn't help stealing a glance back towards him: Iliån had come to a halt at the bottom of his flight of stairs, too. Oliå seized the opportunity presented by a woman walking between them to perform an about-turn and disappear into some hanging dresses. A few moments later, from the safety of a fitting room, she watched him moving through the throng of customers. He had come back upstairs to the floor where she was hiding: he was looking for her. Oliå buried her face in her hands, breathing in the scent of the leather slingshot that never left her wrist. She waited for him to disappear before darting back to the stairway and tearing down it.

When she reached the bottom, she looked up to see him on the third floor, leaning over the handrail and scanning the crowd. She covered her face with the bag of bobbins, fearing she might dissolve into thin air at any second.

Near the entrance, a doorman noticed her acting suspiciously, and stepped in her way.

"Please, mademoiselle," he said, as Oliå flew past him, clinging to her bobbins.

"Mademoiselle!"

Back upstairs, Iliån was looking in their direction.

Oliå pushed open the door and disappeared into the cold.

She never set foot in the department store again, nor did she dare venture close to *Maison Pearl*. She dedicated more time to looking after the elderly Latin teacher; she also swept the floor of a barbershop for a few months, and worked in a greengrocer's. In fact, she was so rushed off her feet it wasn't until the following autumn that she discovered Iliån had left for the war.

One morning, Madame Pearl saw a young girl enter the shop.

"I came for the advertisement," she said.

"Which advertisement would that be, my dear?"

"The advertisement for work."

"There wasn't any advertisement."

"So there isn't any work?"

Esther couldn't deny that there was plenty: her husband had been making deliveries since dawn, and the pair of them had worked all through the night.

"I don't need money," Oliå said. "I want to learn."

"What's your name?"

"Léa."

Madame Pearl advised her to come back the following day. In the evening, she spoke to her husband, who wasn't at all convinced, but Esther asked him to let the

316

girl have a trial before he made any decision.

"Oh, and tell me if you notice anything," she added.

By the end of the next day, Léa had landed the job. She accepted a small wartime salary, and Madame Pearl was very happy with her. At closing time, when she could hear the young girl scrubbing the floor in the backroom, she spoke to her husband in hushed tones.

"So? See what I was talking about?"

"The accent," Pearl replied without a moment's hesitation.

Léa had exactly the same accent as their boy.

For a long time, almost two years, there was no news of the soldier. Then they received the letter. Those two pages all the way from Germany stirred up the memories at *Maison Pearl*. Oliå was happy for them to read the words ten times over, with Jacques Pearl apologizing all the while for going on about the boy so much.

"One day you'll understand, mademoiselle," he said.

But she understood already, and out in the street, when she was delivering a box of marshmallows, Oliå would repeat the name of Joshua – the new name of her love.

She agreed to pose for the photograph they were planning on sending to the prisoner. The Pearls wanted to show him that business was good and that the shop was doing well. Oliå smiled in front of the pharma-cist's camera, but in the photograph there were only her dainty footprints in the snow: she had known for a long time that she left no trace in any photograph.

For that very reason, no counterfeiter had ever managed to provide her with forged identity papers, although it wasn't for lack of trying. Which is why her name didn't feature on a single list, not even the one detailing the men, women and children who were arrested in the summer of 1942.

On the day of the round-up, Oliå arrived late at the shop for the first time ever: the Latin teacher had just died of old age in her bed.

Maison Pearl was deserted, except for the marsh-mallows waiting beneath their layer of muslin. She closed the iron shutter.

Oliå hid herself away for months in the Pearls' apart-ment. She knew that if Joshua was alive, he would return to this place; and so that was where she needed to be.

One night in November, she was woken by the sound of loud knocking. She immediately turned off the lights. It was him. Oliå spent several agonising seconds sitting on the floor with her back against the locked door, painfully aware of his presence behind her.

She was tempted to fling open the door, just for the split second they'd enjoy together. Perhaps she'd even have time to touch his skin. But then she imagined Iliån's overwhelming sense of loneliness the moment after she disappeared.

Oliå didn't hear him leave; she assumed she must have lost him once again. But he returned a little later in the evening. She had pulled the key out of the lock so that he could come in. This time, Joshua wasn't alone: he was with Suzanne. Oliå had just enough time to hide behind the curtain.

He set off, taking one of her blue slippers with him. She decided to follow him, settling in the same village in Provence, where she would play guardian angel. Oliå placed herself at Captain Alexandre's service so that she could keep an eye on her prince. Alexandre was delighted to have such a brilliant operator by his side, and she even dealt with his housework and laundry.

By staying close to the leader, Oliå traced the same path as Iliån: she came to understand what he already understood. *Spells can be undone, but this requires tokens of proof.* On the last day of the war, she gave Joshua the first token, untying from her wrist the only object of his that she'd been able to keep – the sling-shot – and leaving it on the table at the Pilon farm.

For ten years, her hope was renewed. Back in Paris, she kept a close watch on Joshua Pearl's double life, looking on as he prepared for his return to the Kingdoms. She could see that each journey was born of his love for her, and she awaited each and every reappearance in the same way that a wife might. But whenever he returned from his journeys, all she could do was pace the city, keeping her distance from the shop and waiting patiently.

Oliå passed the time. She started reading, and learnt to play the piano. She sat in universities and schools, listening in on the lectures and lessons. She worked for a printer, a goldsmith and a milliner... Everyone was astonished that a girl of fifteen could be so well versed in pre-war fashion. She studied Latin and Greek, and sat as a model for a painter who was fascinated by her. Paintings alone were able to capture her beauty, which could never be photographed.

But nothing lasts in this world. After a few years, people became suspicious of her childish face and her unchanging complexion. The milliner started asking questions. The professors and teachers summoned her to their offices.

"Something's not right," said the painter, catching up with her in the street below his studio. "Please, tell me what's going on."

"I don't know what you're talking about," she replied.

"Mademoiselle, I'm begging you..."

She escaped, running elsewhere, uprooting herself once again. Only Joshua would be able to make all this stop one day.

So she started roaming the area near the shop, and would pay the occasional visit to the apartment when he was away. One night, she even defended the place against thieves by pushing all the cases up behind the door.

In the end though, she lost him.

The first thing Oliå saw was that the lights in *Maison Pearl* were off. Nosy onlookers were gazing in at the broken glass and debris in the shop. She stepped inside. Some of the neighbours were being questioned: nobody knew what had happened. One of them mentioned something about women of easy virtue frequenting the backroom of the shop.

"Not that I knew anything about his personal life,"

the man said, with a discretion that didn't ring true.

"He must have amassed quite a fortune," a lady added.

The police officers walked around indifferently, knocking away bits of plasterwork with their truncheons.

Oliå tiptoed upstairs and found the apartment empty. The archers had ripped up the parquet floor and hacked at the walls in the quest for hidden compartments.

Oliå spent several years searching for him, but in the end she gave up.

She became a dancer, starting from scratch every four years: a young star who lit up the stage for a few seasons, before making her debut again somewhere else. Oliå travelled the world calling herself Rebecca, Salomé, Naomi, Jeanne, Céleste and Claire-Marie.

As I re-read these lines, I realize I could never have imagined myself writing them: words that detail the life of a fairy. Nothing could have prepared me for such familiarity with one of these extraordinary beings.

I always used to put fairies in the same basket as all those other creatures endlessly recycled from the grand bazaar of the magical and the marvellous.

Each of our imaginations is unique and impossible to replicate, or so it seems to me; they are like personal storerooms, or intimate sanctuaries. So it is that – in all of our minds – there are strange creatures, enchanted forests and miniature worlds. What I had never accepted was the idea of fairies or elves moving from inside one head to inside another. Why should we play host to creatures invented by other people?

But stories change us. And there are some encounters that flip us onto our backs like tortoises, forcing us to wake up and listen.

She knew that she would track him down in the end. When it did happen it was completely by chance, thanks to an old dancer in Milan who mentioned that he'd just struck lucky: having picked up a pair of ballet pumps in a second-hand shop and sold them for a fortune to a strange buyer with stormy grey eyes.

Oliå caught up with Pearl as he was preparing to return to France. By following him, she eventually arrived at the house by the river. She waded into the water and spotted him on the bank, his three dogs circling around him.

She settled down not far from there, and made her

living from gathering willow and weaving baskets, just as she had done back in the days when she was a fairy.

Pearl's dogs never sniffed out her presence, and she made the most of this by haunting the grass and reeds by the water's edge. Often she would moor her boat by a washhouse a little further downstream, and bathe amongst the water lilies.

It was here, on the wooden planks of this washhouse, that one autumn morning she saw a fourteen-year-old boy taking photographs of frogs.

Me.

30

The First Book of Pearl

Staring at the washhouse again, twenty-five years later, I thought back to the photograph I had taken that day: the girl standing on her boat, pushing a long pole to propel the vessel laden with branches, and allowing herself to be photographed with an ease that suited me. Her lack of self-consciousness had been startling.

Now the washhouse was half-demolished, and the same went for Joshua Pearl's house downriver, together with most of my memories. The sole witness was an old man with a luminous quality, and he was almost certainly buried in the grave alongside the house.

But then there was the box, which had bizarrely appeared on the doormat the previous day. I'd left it behind in Paris, hidden in the cupboard that used to serve as our darkroom. The box – and only the box – could shed some light on all of this: why had I let myself be separated from it?

That evening, back in my mother's apartment, I dug it out from under the winter coats. Everything was still there. I shook the canisters gently against my ear, to check the rolls of films were still inside.

Then I headed back to join my family for the rest of our holiday, the box weighing heavy on my back. They gave me a warm welcome, without any reproaches or big displays of emotion. The world had carried on without me. Why expect flags and parades and processions, as if returning triumphantly from battle, when no one could possibly know what I'd just experienced?

Sometimes, in the middle of a meal, I would get up and check that the box was still there, under the washbasin in the bathroom.

There was just one shop in the nearest town that developed old films, and the owner appeared tickled by the small relics I brought in.

"Grandma passed away, has she?" he enquired, immediately assuming that I'd found the films stashed in the furniture of a dead relative. I informed him I was the one who'd taken the photos, and that I was very much alive. I chuckled to prove my point.

"I only used four of the films. But take all seven, because I'm not sure which are which."

Pushing my luck, I also took out the two Super 8 cartridges from my bag.

He held them at arm's length, as if they were pieces of debris from a meteorite, then handed them straight back, no explanation needed.

He asked me to settle the bill in advance, because sometimes he ended up with unwanted photos.

"I can hardly display them in my living room, now can I?"

The printing process would take an eternity. The films had to be transferred to some faraway photo lab, and would then be posted back to the shop. The man said he would ring me when they were ready. In the meantime, after searching online, I'd sent the two Super 8 cartridges to an address in Germany. They promised to return them within five weeks.

Both sets of deadlines felt inhuman. Koala bears give birth after five weeks; and in half that time, it's possible to circumnavigate the globe in a hot air balloon. What were the developers going to do with my images for five whole weeks? Lose them a hundred times?

To make matters worse, the shop didn't call me back. I was convinced they'd misplaced the films and weren't sure how to break the news to me. Eventually

I paid them another visit, only to be told that everything was in order and that perhaps I might like to try exercising some patience.

Two days later, while I was slicing aubergines in the kitchen, a message came through on my phone: the photos were ready for me to pick up. I nearly chopped off my finger.

I was back in the shop within the hour, and the lady behind the counter duly produced the package.

"Would you like to check them here?"

"No thanks."

She gave me the price.

"I already settled up with your male colleague, the other day."

She examined the package and the bill.

"You paid for four films."

"Yes."

"But there are seven. They developed all seven."

"All seven?"

"Would you like to check?"

"No, thank you."

My brain was in overdrive as I held out the money with trembling hands: Pearl must have used the camera and the last rolls of film in my absence.

* * *

I didn't head straight back to my family, but stopped the car in the hills and walked a while until I found a suitable spot. I thought back to all the important letters that I'd received in my life, and how I liked to take my time choosing where to read them, as if the landscape could alter the content.

By chance, the first two packages were in the right order.

The first film showed my family, with my brothers, my little sister and even the gutters on our apartment. They were meant to be "arty" photographs, with a whimsical composition, but the blurriness was only partly intentional. You didn't need to be an expert in photography to spot how bad they were, but the context made them touching: memories that had incubated inside a plastic egg for twenty-five years, suddenly seeing the light of day...

The three last photos in the wallet had been taken on the train on my way to the photography course. They were brilliantly blurry.

The second film captured the first two days of my adventure, starting with a few hens, a close-up portrait of a chick that looked like it was grinning, and a leek placed on a table next to a carrot. I had been under orders to find my subject. I'd tried this and that, nearly settling on a contrived scene involving my bicycle high up in a tree.

But most of the ensuing photos were of the water and the river. Some made me regret giving up on the idea of a career in photography at around the age of fifteen and a half. Then, when I saw the first frogs appear, I felt a lump in my throat. We were approaching the apparition.

I lifted the flap of the third wallet, before quickly closing it again. I had just seen a dead dog. I knew I wasn't mistaken: the image I had glimpsed was of a big black dog lying on its back, with a bloodstain on its fur. I trembled as I put the wallet down. This wasn't my third film.

My heart was racing in the same way it had on those rare occasions when I'd been confronted with a snake: I had the same sensation of everything inside me collapsing. I stared at the closed wallets for several minutes.

In the end, I picked one up – not the right one – and it triggered an altogether different emotion. Relief.

This package was my victory. It contained all the photographs I'd taken in Pearl's absence. The house at daybreak; the crayfish on the pontoon; and, above all, those suitcases crammed with treasure. I found myself back there, with the treasure spread out in front of me, wrapped in white tissue paper, and yet I was entirely unaware that for Pearl these represented tokens from the Kingdoms. Selfishly, I only saw the proof of my own history. I had been in that house. I had met that man. That was all I wanted to know.

Perhaps I should have stopped there. But I picked up the fourth wallet, which dated back to a few days earlier. In front of me was the last photo of a frog on the washhouse and, in the background, a boat approaching. I flicked through the images one by one: the bundles of branches; the pole planted in the water lilies; the grey sky reflected in the waterlogged bottom of the boat...

It was all there, except for her. If the girl had disappeared, then the snake had slithered back under my feet. Where had my muse gone? No memory was so deeply etched into my mind. I could recall every second of what should have been captured in these photographs. I could picture the angle of her knee beneath the fabric of her dress; the way her hand had framed the wooden pole; the green trousers she wore on the last day; and the flower in her hair too. Except that there was no flower, or dress, or trousers – just an empty river.

I wanted to find a satisfactory reason, perhaps a chemical or meteorological explanation. It had rained heavily during those final days. Had the negatives been damaged by the bad weather? I blamed the photo lab as well: the process had taken too long... They must have done something underhand with my photographs... Perhaps they were playing a mean trick on me?

I stood up and let out the same cry as years earlier when I was lost in the woods. A cry of defiance that railed against the world. Afterwards, sitting back down with the last three films, I began with the images of the dead dog: one of Pearl's handsome hounds, lying on its back in the thick grass. I took my time, examining the rest of the photographs, until I reached the final one. There were exactly one hundred of them.

It took me more than a year.

I told people I had embarked on a project; one that required a lot of research. I called it *The Book of Pearl* and the way I described it was so confusing they had no choice but to trust me.

At the beginning, my days all followed the same pattern. I would spread the photographs out on the ground in a square, ten by ten, and would walk around it.

Those one hundred photographs told the tale of an odyssey. They had been taken by Joshua Pearl from the very first day that he'd borrowed my camera. Picking up on the few clues that helped me date some of them, I soon realized that they spanned over twenty years. So he had only taken four or five photos a year.

While I was growing up, while we were getting on with our lives, Pearl had spent his time fleeing different parts of the world. Each image was another chapter that told the story of an epic voyage involving hundreds of suitcases. His nomadic life seemed unreal.

Those suitcases were well travelled. I saw them sliding across snowfields, waiting by the sea, crossing rivers. They were piled up inside stables or beneath tents. In one photograph, the mound of leather, wood and waxed canvas was hidden high in a tree in the corner of a field. And then there were strange images: a few suitcases carried off by the current; others waiting on a barren mountainside beside two donkeys.

As I worked on the project, and the weeks went by, I felt like a character in a fairy tale; except that instead of following a trail of breadcrumbs or pebbles out of the dark woods, I was wandering from one photo to another as I tried to piece together the story.

The two films, which I finally managed to see on an

old projector, each lasted three minutes. They hardly showed anything, but they had a profound effect on me. I had filmed the first one on the river, and then in and around the house. The second was taken by Pearl. It showed a dog running through the grass, and a raft piled with suitcases, being pulled through the water by a boat.

The first thing that struck me about my square of one hundred photographs was the dwindling number of suitcases. The journey was marked by loss; so my narrative had to be about the struggle against time and death. Towards the end, in the final photographs, the pile of luggage formed a perfect cube, pulled tight inside a net. There were still two dogs at the beginning, but one by one they disappeared in turn.

The last photograph was of the bow of a boat. Pearl had succeeded in returning to port: that much I could see. His quest was meant to finish where it had begun, in the house by the water's edge. For a storyteller, coming full circle in this way was ideal. I had even seen Pearl's grave, close to the house, with my own eyes. The adventurer had returned to die in the place where he had lived.

It was all perfect.

During the winter, I set off in search of various places, in order to conduct my research more thoroughly. In the middle of nowhere, I found the remains of the old Citroën cattle truck that could be seen in the first photos. I tracked down the landscapes, villages and beaches. I was walking in Pearl's footsteps.

Late one evening, I printed out a ream of paper and set it down on my table. I had finished.

Next to my manuscript were the one hundred photographs. I felt an overwhelming sense of relief. *The Book of Pearl* was somewhere between a fable and an adventure story. At last, I was ready for someone else to read the pages that had liberated me from my memories, and from the ghost of the girl.

But in the middle of the night, one of the images woke me with a start. It was the second photograph in the first row. I stole quietly out of bed and went to take a look at it on the table, picking up the image that came just after the one with the dead dog.

I called this photo "Farewell to the House", because it came at the start of the adventure. The house and the pontoon had been photographed from the boat. Inspecting it more closely, I noticed a tiny detail I hadn't spotted before. There, against the wall, in the long grass, was the grave.

The grave was already there.

So I had got everything wrong from beginning to end; all my hard work was going up in smoke. Either Pearl hadn't taken any of the photographs himself, or this wasn't his grave. And a man with no grave might very well be alive.

The day after that sleepless night, I received an anonymous note in the post: a few lines setting the time and place for a meeting three days later. The message ended with a question that was repeated, in small and then capital letters:

> *What do you think you're doing?*
> *WHAT ARE YOU DOING?*

The note was written on white paper from *Maison Pearl*.

31

AN APPARITION

The house was right in the middle of Venice, although only a few of its windows overlooked a small canal. The address given in the message was for a waterfront entrance, but I was determined to arrive on foot rather than by boat. I knew nothing about this meeting. What if it was a trap, and I needed to make a hasty getaway?

Looking back on it now, the dangers I imagined were far smaller than those that really did hover around me that day; dangers which had been threatening me, without my knowing it, for months.

And so I had naively gone in search of street access to the rear of the yellow house, with the result that I had taken at least ten wrong turns. Venice is described as a labyrinth, but it's more like two or three labyrinths that have merged with the sole purpose of making you lose your way.

While I was waiting for the appointed hour, I'd already walked past the door once to scope it out. I lingered at the end of the narrow little street, checking my watch. It was Sunday and almost noon. In the distance came the sounds of a motorboat from a wider canal, a cat wailing, ringing bells, and a woman's heels.

I had just spent three days in a tailspin. This had involved destroying my manuscript, reading and re-reading my note of summons, purchasing a ticket for Venice (before nearly binning that as well) and lying to everybody. I had re-opened all the wounds I had painstakingly stitched up with the pages I had been writing for months on end. In a few moments, I might actually discover what all this was about.

The doorbell didn't work when I pressed it, and the door had sunk to lower than head-level. I stared at the rust-coloured mark tracing the outline of the door-frame on the stone. After twenty seconds, I pressed the button again; but this time, in an effort to look more calm and collected, I took a step backwards, thrust my hands into my pockets and swivelled on my heels. Glancing up, I saw a white curtain flap at a window, despite there being no breeze that day. Four small windows were scattered at random across the long vertical façade, and it was out of the top one that the white sail had briefly billowed.

I scanned the other windows, searching for any sign of life. When I looked down again, I discovered that the door was wide open. A half-person stood in the gloom, almost invisible, sliced lengthways by the edge of the door. The inside of the house was pitch black.

As I crossed the threshold, we brushed lightly against one another and I wondered whether this person might be a child. I could feel the first stair underfoot, and my shoulders brushed against the walls of the narrow staircase. Behind me, the patter of bare feet was reassuring. No one was going to chop me into pieces in front of a child.

The stairwell emerged into a room lit up by a window. I could see two chairs, a table, two glasses and a carafe of water. Nothing else. No sign of my mysterious correspondent.

I took in the scene: the frame of light, the small square room, the terracotta tiles, the carafe of water gleaming as in an old painting. I wanted to ask my guide to inform the person who'd summoned me that I'd arrived. But as I turned to speak, I sensed the child passing behind my back, and so I continued my movement until I'd come full circle. And then stopped abruptly.

It was her. She was filling both glasses from the carafe.

It was the girl.

My legs felt as if they were about to give way, and the short distance to the chair suddenly looked unfeasible. But this was only the first wave of shock, for I had yet to notice her age. She wasn't a single day or night older than when she had abandoned me.

I was like a cat that had slipped off a roof now; but as I fell through the air, an unstoppable machine had been set in motion inside me. I'd had this feeling before, when I'd opened the wallets of photos for the first time. It was a machine that made the impossible possible, and it was now consuming all my energy as I frantically tried to work out the logic and reason behind this apparition. Spinning through the void, I cared about just one thing: like any cat in the world, I wanted to land on my feet.

And land on them I did, by uttering the only words that made any sense; the only words that could explain almost everything; the only words that could make me feel the ground beneath my feet.

"Please tell your mother I'm here."

Nothing else could explain such an uncanny resemblance after all these years. The girl in front of me *had* to be her daughter.

As she listened to my pathetic stammering, she pressed a hand into the back of her chair with a weariness that implied it was her who had got the wrong person. My throat tightened in the presence of such sadness. This time, I recognized her. It really was her. In my head, I was switching worlds.

I ventured a step forward and sat down on one of the chairs. The girl stayed standing behind hers. Slowly, we drank in the sight of one another, only looking away to gasp for air. I needed those seconds to come back down to earth.

Eventually, she sat on the other chair in her wide silk trousers, and slid one of the glasses towards her on the table saying, "You're no use to me at all."

I had been through too much by this stage to feel surprised. Instead, I adopted the expression of a child who knew he was in the wrong, and she continued.

"Didn't you receive the package?"

I nodded, guilty again, but of what I had no idea.

"Well?" she asked. "What are you doing?"

That was the central question: the one that was on my note of summons. The one I still didn't understand.

"What do you do?" she asked again.

"What do you mean?"

"What is it that you do?"

"I write," I muttered.

"Sorry?"

"I write."

I must have looked a sorry sight, but she stared at me without any pity. She stood up to half-close the shutters, which I hadn't noticed up until that point. Then she sat down again.

"So you haven't understood anything, then?" she asked softly.

"Nothing at all." I had to admit, after pretending to mull over the question.

And it was the truth.

She drank her glass of water in one.

"They come in twos and threes. They're here, the ones who are after him."

"Who?"

"They're after me too."

"Who's after you?"

She didn't answer.

"He's very old. He can't run away any more."

"Who?" I repeated, before attempting to answer my own question. "Pearl?"

She nodded and, for the first time, I felt that I was truly on a level with her. Emboldened by this, I asked,

"Who are you?"

She poured herself a fresh glass of water, and then she began to talk.

What I've written down here is exactly as she told it to me, from the very first word. It's a story I would never have dared to make up myself. As I listened to the girl, I was thinking back to the pages I had thrown out the day before – the ones that referred to a mad old wanderer – and I realized what had driven me to destroy my story. There were two elements missing: urgency and necessity. Whereas these were at the very heart of her story.

The hours came and went, with deaths and loves floating on a lake; with wild boars in the snow; with a weasel on the ramparts; and with a pair of banished lovers.

Night was falling. The carafe had to be refilled several times. I stayed there, alone, in the middle of the story when she went for more water. I felt cold while she was away. I strained my ears to catch the patter of her footsteps when she was above me, or the sound of running water and then the tap being turned off.

She always came back.

When she spoke of our encounter on the river,

there were long silences between her words. She was watching for my reaction. I could tell she didn't want to hurt me.

By the time I met him in the house guarded by his dogs, Pearl had been collecting for forty years. And Oliå, having finally tracked him down to his hideout, was coming to the realization that he would never stop. He could never have enough tokens of proof, because he was too afraid of not being believed. And so he continued to amass his treasure, in the knowledge that he wouldn't be given a second chance.

"He was afraid," she echoed.

I could picture him again with his nose buried in his ledgers, rearranging his suitcases a thousand times, climbing those ladders.

"And then one morning, at the washhouse, I saw you photographing frogs."

She smiled gently.

"I promise you, I nearly fell in love."

I smiled back, tears in my eyes.

"But you were photographing me for nothing."

She began to laugh.

"Really, for nothing."

She stopped.

"I saw your camera, though, and I thought that

you could take more important photographs. That you could show the tokens of proof."

I looked away, trying not to feel sad, but with little success.

"I told you I have no special powers..."

She was keeping something back.

"But there is one power I'll never lose. You don't need to have been what I was to possess it."

She was speaking in more of a hush now, barely audible.

"The power to make people sad."

A long silence followed.

I understood it was her grief that had led me towards Pearl; the same heartbreak had led us both through the woods. I realized too that she had returned to open the suitcases and play at being a small ghost in the house by the river in order to pique my curiosity. It was because of her that I had photographed some of the treasure.

But Pearl had caught me red-handed with my camera, and kept me at a distance for a very long time.

Oliå pronounced the name Iliån by elongating the "a", as if it were a sigh. She only had to say his name once for me to understand how much she loved him. I could never measure up to that.

When she began to speak again, she told me about the attack. An archer had finally located the house, four years after my stay there. Pearl was away on his travels. An arrow had killed one of the dogs, and the other two hounds had thrown themselves on the man. Oliå arrived too late to save the archer, but before he died she made him speak of the Kingdoms.

The archer had been sent by Iån. Back in their realm, the keeper of the lightship had eventually denounced Taåg, so Iån knew that his brother and Oliå were alive somewhere; and that Iliån was preparing his return.

Their aged father had long since died. And Fåra, the old servant, must have disappeared as well.

Once Iån had done with wreaking havoc and dereliction in the Kingdoms, and bringing his own people to their knees, he proceeded to send his mercenaries even further afield. The first archer arrived in our world on a summer's evening. He died in an accident in the canals of Bruges, but ever since then there'd been plenty more on the hunt for Iliån. And one of them had been running across the rooftops of Venice for two days now.

Night had fallen and I could no longer see Oliå; I could only hear her feet sliding over the floor beneath her chair. She confided that she always carried the bow she had taken from the first archer.

"What about the grave close to the house?" I wanted to know.

"It was for one of his dogs."

"What do you want from me?"

"I found you dancing in that place."

"At the fire station? I wasn't dancing."

She laughed very softly.

"You fainted."

I didn't want to admit that I had probably collapsed after glimpsing her for a split second in the crowd.

"I followed you in order to give you the box."

"So it was you?"

When she answered, it was in a very different voice.

"Iliån will die soon. You have all the tokens of proof. You must write our story."

I couldn't believe my ears: she wanted me to reverse the spell that had been cast over them.

I couldn't tell her that the person she was addressing was not the same as the fourteen-year-old boy she had known before; and that between then and now I had forfeited everyone's trust, because I told stories for a living.

Quite simply, nobody would believe me.

"What about you?" I asked.

"My fate is intertwined with his. I shall return with him."

She told me about those youthful, lifeless bodies, which had been hidden together within the cliff-face, above the lightship. They had been waiting to be awoken for nearly a century. I tried to picture their small tomb in amongst the swallows' nests.

"Where is Pearl?" I asked.

"Here in Venice."

"I want to speak to him."

32

THE ETERNAL PALACE

When Attila and his armies invaded Europe, the refugees that were routed from the torched cities of northern Italy fled to a group of marshes and small sandy islands. There they built huts on top of the wooden stakes they had driven into the muddy terrain. Hidden in this deserted lagoon, they were safe from marauding horsemen and ships raiding the coastline. In time, this place would become Venice.

One and a half thousand years later, Joshua Pearl had washed up in this corner of the world for the same reason.

And now here I was, standing at a distance and staring at a small palace, its stonework held in place by an outer layer of wooden planks and beams to prevent it from collapsing. It looked like Noah's ark.

Oliå had told me that it was sinking into the sea,

and that nobody was able to go inside any more. At the time I didn't believe her, but now I could see she was right: the house must have sunk by two or three metres in the last few years. At water level, there was just the top of a door and some windows where the river rushed in. The upper floors were waiting their turn behind the wooden carapace.

I carried out my first check at nine o'clock in the morning. Since the night before, I'd felt a little unsettled, as though I were straddling two worlds. There was the world that existed beneath my feet and in the air around me: the cobblestones of Venice's quaysides, the wind, the aroma of coffee and the scent of jasmine in the streets. And then there was the other one: that of the story world, the Kingdoms that the girl had granted me a glimpse of, and which appeared all the more real because it was new to me.

I felt feverish, weightless, all at sea.

Oliå's instructions were to wait until the following night before entering Pearl's house, but she'd also advised me to scout the premises beforehand. She went to great pains to stress the precautions I needed to take: play the tourist, don't stop outside the palace and use the maze of streets and alleys to shake off the enemy.

The enemy. I'd quivered with pleasure on hearing

that word: Oliå was putting me in the same camp as her. For the first time, we shared a common enemy. We stood together.

But after I'd left her to pace the streets by myself, and as the shutters started to bang in the evening wind, I remembered the blood-soaked arrows of the archers, and suddenly I was less keen on our enemies.

The following afternoon, I returned for one last look. She had mentioned a walkway to me, and this time I spotted it. There were some wooden beams running along the façade just below the waterline, and it looked possible to walk along them barefoot in order to reach a small square of planks nailed together that I could see higher up. Oliå had told me that this was in fact an opening which lifted up like a catflap; from time to time she would secretly leave a basket of supplies there for Pearl. She said that if a basket or a cat could fit through the gap, then so could I, which didn't strike me as being entirely logical.

Once night had fallen, I found myself squeezed in amongst the other passengers on the boat that was bringing me closer to Pearl. I was thinking back to the fourteen-year-old boy who had followed the trail of blood into the dark woods one day. That boy was me. That trail had in fact been left by me. And perhaps today was just another instance of me inventing mysteries.

I tallied up the proof I had at my disposal. There was almost none: only a girl who resembled another girl, some photographs of a few suitcases and an epic story deep within me.

It was almost midnight, and the other passengers were returning from dinner. Their laughter filled the boat. For them, the party was still in full swing. I wasn't the only one drifting between two worlds. Each of them had their own secrets, their own stories that nobody else believed. Was there a single being on-board who could honestly say they'd never fallen in love with a fairy or a banished prince? We were all the same. Stories create us.

But I was the only person to disembark at the next stop; the boat danced on merrily.

I often thought about the last of those hundred photographs, the one that showed the bow of a boat. I'd assumed this was a return to the source; to the house on the river. What I hadn't realized was that the boat was bound for Venice.

I made a few obligatory detours down alleyways and over bridges, before stopping in front of the palace. With a final glance to check the dark-windowed houses, the water and quays around me, I pulled off my shoes and slid one foot onto the submerged walkway. The only lantern was a hundred metres ahead, but I could just see my feet in the inky water below. I approached the flap and immediately realized I wasn't going to fit through.

What happened in the next few seconds meant I had no time to come up with another plan. Something fell from the sky just above me, followed by two tiny splashes at my feet. Were they tiles tumbling from the roof? Either that or they were arrows. I didn't wait to find out, launching myself into the canal and swimming along to find another way into the building.

I groped around and soon discovered a submerged window frame: I tucked my head in, dived down and pulled my body through it. When I emerged on the other side, gasping for breath, everything was pitch black. I realized I must be inside the palace, in the middle of a room that had been flooded by the canal. I had to keep kicking so that my head stayed above water. The whole experience reminded me of my first encounter with Pearl in the rushing river: the dark, the cold, the fear.

I still didn't know whether I had fled from arrows or roof tiles, but whatever they were, someone had been responsible for them falling. Someone was besieging the palace.

Swimming clumsily, I managed to edge my way along one of the walls. My body was stiff with exhaustion, and I couldn't find anything to cling on to. Eventually, after fumbling just below the surface, I found an opening. I was reluctant to go any further into this crumbling wreck, but in the end I had little choice other than to dive down again and be guided by the arched ceiling of a corridor. As I pushed aside the floating chairs and other bits of scattered debris, the passage suddenly widened.

I felt as if I were suffocating, and thrust my head out of the water. That's when I saw him.

He was standing, slingshot in hand, towards the top of a stone staircase that opened into a vast room. At his feet blazed a large pot filled with oil or pitch, that lit up his face as he stared at me floundering in the water.

Despite the inevitable signs of the passing of time, it was what hadn't changed about him that fascinated me the most. He was the same man, with the same look in his eyes. I pulled myself up onto the steps below him.

"Don't you recognize me?"

But Pearl didn't answer. I could see a lead pellet the

size of a fist in his slingshot.

"A long time ago, I came to your house. The photographs, the dogs... Do you remember?"

"You took back the box?"

"I was given it."

"By whom?"

Ever since the first day, Pearl had known there was someone in his shadow. He had learnt not to be surprised by it. But why did his guardian angel insist on putting this boy in his path every twenty-five years? He crouched down to look at me.

I was cold, my clothes were clinging to my body and my shoes were nowhere to be seen. I could tell that Pearl was trying to understand, to glean some usefulness from this spluttering creature that kept on dropping into his life, like a fly in his soup.

As the wind whistled through the palace, Pearl looked up, listening to each sound in the dark.

"They've found me," he murmured. "For a long time, they sent men in twos or threes. I escaped every time. But today, there's one up there who has found me."

He rolled the slingshot around his wrist.

"This one is taking his time. He paces across the surrounding rooftops. He's been preparing for at least four days. He's alone. He's different. He means to be the last."

Pearl carried on up the staircase and I followed him, discovering the house as I went. Burning pots marked a path between walls lined with shadowy silk. Oliå had described in great detail the summer palace where it had all begun, but this was an eternal palace. I could understand why someone would choose to shut himself in here forever. Each room opened onto the next in long vertical vistas of steep staircases and vaulted ceilings patterned with gold.

The palace was marvellous to behold: as dark and enclosed as a tomb, brimming with alcoves, upholstered seats and beds hidden away in velvet dens. I felt guilty walking around barefoot, embarrassed about my sodden clothes dripping on the carpets. I followed Pearl into the great hall, and it was then that I saw the suitcases.

There were far fewer than before. They formed a cube, pulled tight inside the fisherman's net I recognized from the photographs. This was all that remained of his treasure trove; all he'd been able to salvage after so many years on the run. These were his tokens of proof from the story world. And his evidence that fairies exist.

Pearl passed behind the enormous linen curtain that divided the room in half. Behind him, two tall windows extended from floor to ceiling. Their panes, boarded up with planks on the outside, glinted in the light of the torches.

I had joined him on the other side of the curtain. From the window, he removed a triangle of glass no larger than his hand, and gently pushed one of the planks aside. A draft raised the linen curtain.

"He's here. He's coming in now," Pearl said, turning round.

I took a step back, not quite understanding.

It was as if the old man were seeing a ghost as he watched the curtain flapping above the floor.

"The draft means that someone has forced an opening elsewhere in the palace."

He turned to look at me.

"When my dogs rescued you all those years ago, I thought about telling you everything..."

His eyes seemed to fill with regret.

"I know almost everything now," I tried to reassure him.

He hadn't moved.

"I know about the clouds of mosquitoes on the lake, about your brother Iån, about the storm that brought you into this world, and about *Maison Pearl* in Paris…"

No sooner had I said the word "storm" than a first clap of thunder resounded behind the windows.

"Who sent you?"

"You need to tell me the parts I don't know. That's why I've come."

We were back by the suitcases on the far side of the curtain. He looked at me with a weariness I had never expected to read on his face.

"It's too late now."

In the space of three seconds, the three torches lighting up the room were extinguished. All that remained was the glow from behind the curtain.

The fourth arrow was aimed at Joshua Pearl.

33

The Last Archer

He ducked and rolled to one side as the arrow flew just over our heads. Pearl dragged me backwards behind some paintings propped against the wall, forming a sort of makeshift tunnel at floor level. From our canvas hideout, the archer was nowhere to be seen.

"I am old," whispered Pearl. "I won't be able to fight for much longer. But you must stay alive."

"I'll help you," I replied.

"The only way you can help me is by staying alive."

I sensed from the desperation in Pearl's voice that he thought nothing could return him to the Kingdoms now. When a man dies he takes with him the spells that were cast on him, unless those spells are undone beforehand. And Pearl thought he was about to die.

But he did have one hope: that this story of love and exile, this story with its unhappy ending, might one day be told. Stories can't bring back the dead, but they can make their love immortal.

I felt his hand gripping my arm, and I realized that he was willing to risk anything.

"Don't move," he said.

"You must stay alive too. I know she's waiting for you in the Kingdoms."

He stared at me for a moment as if I were the one from another world; as if I – and not he – had fallen from the sky one stormy evening. Then he flung himself through a hail of arrows towards the suitcases.

The archer had extinguished the torches in the great hall so that we could no longer see him, but he had a clear view of his target: Pearl was silhouetted against the thin linen curtain that divided the room into two equal halves.

I wanted to go behind this screen and extinguish the last sources of light: the dark would help Pearl escape his assassin. But just as I was about to leave my hiding place, I saw the archer slide closer. He hadn't noticed me, but I could see his silhouette on the other side of the curtain, which was glowing like a yellow screen.

The storm was rumbling outside, shaking the wooden planks which clanked against the walls of the palace. The archer scoured the room, his bow slung across his body, his sword drawn and glinting in the twilight.

Suddenly, I saw Joshua Pearl stand up behind the pile of suitcases. He was holding an altogether flimsier weapon, a sort of musketeer's fencing foil that I remember photographing at the house by the river. The two men stared at each other. Pearl stepped forward and began to speak in a language I didn't understand, but which sprang from his lips like a poem.

The other man remained silent. With his chest thrust forward and his blade pointing at the floor, Pearl appeared to be challenging him to a fair fight.

He uttered a few more of those strange words, while the unknown assassin had his back to the glowing curtain. Although I couldn't see the archer's face, he seemed to be as old as Pearl. He lowered his sword in what I thought to be a sign of peace. Then, just as calmly, he moved his bow into position, plucked an arrow from his back and fitted it on the string, which he pulled taut towards him. He took aim.

The arrow embedded itself in Pearl's arm, and his stage sword clattered to the floor, his eyes burning with pain. He watched as the archer methodically prepared his second arrow. I was numb with horror, incapable even of crying out.

How can I describe what happened next? I can only say that it felt like divine justice.

One of the two floor-length windows suddenly shattered behind the curtain. The room filled with the sounds of thunder, splintering wood and shattered glass, as the rain came sluicing in sideways.

The archer was rooted to the spot. Behind him, the light was dancing across the screen.

I thought the whole of heaven was wreaking its vengeance, but no, it was a living shadow that entered with this hurricane: a shadow cast by the torch still blazing behind the linen curtain; the shadow of a diminutive dancer that I alone recognized.

Oliå had leapt from a rooftop on the opposite side of the canal to hurl herself against the palace's worm-eaten exterior. Crashing through the wood and glass, she plunged into the midst of the chaos.

She was the avenging angel.

Pearl was still on his feet, his sleeve soaked in blood. He had torn the arrow from his arm, and was now watching the shadow-play projected onto the curtain.

The archer had turned to discover that the dancer's shadow was also armed with a bow. But no sooner was he aiming to release another arrow through the fabric, than the shape dissolved on the white screen.

With a mighty kick, Oliå had knocked over the only remaining torch and sent it rolling underneath the curtain to the other side, where it came to a halt behind the assassin's feet. The flame kept on burning, and now the archer's shadow, not Oliå's, was framed on the curtain like a target. His bow was still drawn back, but he no longer had any idea where to aim.

And at that very moment I saw the tip of an arrow pierce the linen from the other side, right in the middle of the shadow. It burst through the fabric with a faint ripping sound and raced towards the archer.

Oliå had aimed for the heart.

The archer remained upright for a few seconds, then collaspsed. As his body foundered, he snuffed out the last torch. A little further away I could barely make out Pearl, who had himself fallen to his knees.

But a spark from the torch had set the great linen curtain ablaze, and it was burning now from the bottom up like a sheet of paper. I felt as though I were seeing a theatre curtain rise, as the stage lights came up. In a matter of seconds, Oliå would appear before Pearl's eyes and everything would be over. It was imperative he didn't see her.

When the curtain had finished burning, all that could be seen was a deserted battlefield, a bow lying on the rubble and a shattered window. Ash was raining down, but the fire hadn't spread to the wooden beams.

I ran towards the window and leant out. The storm was still raging over the city. As a bolt of lightning lit up the sky, just below me I could see a tiny patch of white foam. She had dived in. I imagined her breathing hard as she swam, her body darting through the murky water.

Pearl had crawled over to the archer, and I went to join him in the flickering light of the storm. He was deep in thought next to the body, and seemed to have forgotten about his wounded arm.

I crouched beside him and whispered, "You said he was the last archer."

"Yes."

"So the war is over," I said. "He's dead."

"Yes."

We stayed there for several minutes with the wind and rain lashing through the window.

"How do you know he was the last?" I asked.

His hands were spread on the wooden floor next to the white hair on the dead man's head.

"Because he was my brother."

* * *

All of a sudden, as if in a dream, I saw a land freed from its tyrant; a realm whose ravaged people were waiting on the shoreline opposite an abandoned palace. And I could see, high up on a cliffface, a cave open to the sea, with the motionless bodies of two fifteen year olds, one beside the other. Iliån and Oliå.

As you read these words, something has moved in the windswept tomb. Their hands are not yet touching, but their lips part to let in the air. Their nostrils flare and catch the scent of the saffron that clings to the rocks. And, if you're willing to believe me, the two bodies will soon be stretching out their stiff limbs and each will hear the sound of the other breathing.

They are about to open their eyes. He watches as she turns her whole body towards him. They bide their time a while yet. How long have they been asleep?

The prince has now reached the age when he can become king. In a moment, the girl will at last begin to grow older, in accordance with the slow passage of time in the fairytale world.

Together they will rebuild a palace of reeds by the lake, with walls of woven willow; and in winter the surface will ice over so that herds of reindeer can cross it.

In the evenings, they will tell stories to their children

who have rowed home across the lake, after building dams among the irises by the source. Stories of kingdoms like their own: the tale of a cat and his boots, of a girl with a bright red hood, or a king driven mad by grief. But their favourite ones will always come from a far-off world inhabited by marshmallow-sellers, a land of wars and creaking crayfish beneath wooden pontoons.

This is what I dreamt as I witnessed old Joshua Pearl next to the dead brother who was a stranger to him. I knew that all this would take time to come true. How was I to tell their story? How was I to make people believe it?

Perhaps Oliå would stay for a while in her tiny house in Venice, and Iliån too in the palace that was being reclaimed by water. He would have to carry his suitcases up to the attic to save them.

Would I have the time and the words to restore them to their realm? That now depended on me.

I left and I set to work. All I had kept of the destroyed manuscript was the title, *The Book of Pearl*.

The rest is here.

At times, I felt as if the words from my pen were tracing a path from one page to the next; a path that would lead Iliån and Oliå back home. The more I wrote, the further their lantern disappeared into the ink as black as the night sky. I knew that when I wrote the final word, they would no longer be here.

And so I paused for a moment, just before finishing.

I wasn't sure whether to weep or smile as I imagined them together for ever, so far away from me.

READ OTHER BOOKS BY

TIMOTHÉE DE FOMBELLE...

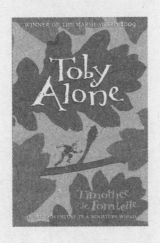

TOBY ALONE

He's just one and a half millimetres tall, but Toby Lolness is the most wanted person in the great oak Tree. Pursued across a hazardous terrain of falling leaves, thick moss forests and bark mountains, hunted by an army of angry woodcutters and bloodthirsty soldier ants, Toby faces an epic battle for survival in an unforgettable miniature world.

"To take one tree as emblematic and bring it alive in great detail is imaginatively rich and great fun." *Guardian*

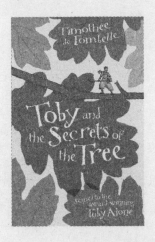

TOBY AND THE SECRETS
OF THE TREE

The world of the great oak Tree is on the brink
of devastation under the control of the power-
crazed Leo Blue. Leo is inflicting fear and
poverty throughout the Tree, capturing anyone
who tries to resist and destroying the very bark
on which they live. But Toby has returned –
and he will find a way to fight back.

"You'll never look at a tree in the same way
again... An unprecedented success." *Le Figaro*

Vango, Book One: Between Sky and Earth

Fleeing from the police and more sinister forces
on his trail, Vango must race against time to prove
his innocence – a journey that will take him to the
farthest reaches of distant lands. Can Vango uncover
the secrets of his past before everything is lost?

"Exciting, unusual and beautifully written."
David Almond

Vango, Book Two: A Prince Without a Kingdom

Vango has spent his life abandoning his loved ones to protect them from the demons of his past. But the mystery of his identity has started to unravel, and in the shadows of war and persecution, the truth will finally come to light.

"A distinctive and atmospherically cinematic tale."
Independent

Sarah Ardizzone (née Adams) is one of the most sought-after translators working today. She has won several awards for her work, including twice receiving the Marsh Award for children's literature in translation: in 2009 for *Toby Alone* by Timothée de Fombelle and in 2005 for *Eye of the Wolf* by Daniel Pennac. Sarah promotes translation as a creative process in schools and beyond.

Sam Gordon is the translator of *Arab Jazz* by Karim Miské, which won a 2014 English PEN award and was also shortlisted for a CWA International Dagger in 2015. He recently translated *Captain Rosalie*, a short story by Timothée de Fombelle, which appeared in *The Great War: Stories Inspired by Objects from the First World War*. Alongside his literary translation work, Sam teaches French.

Timothée de Fombelle is a celebrated author and playwright who achieved international success with his stunning debut, *Toby Alone*, and its sequel, *Toby and the Secrets of the Tree*. The series was translated into 28 languages and has won numerous awards, including France's prestigious Prix Sorcières and the Marsh Award for children's literature in translation. His gripping mystery-adventure series, *Vango, Between Sky and Earth* and *Vango, A Prince Without a Kingdom* gained international praise, and the first novel received an English Pen Award for translation. More recently, Timothée wrote a compelling short story called *Captain Rosalie*, which appeared in the critically acclaimed anthology *The Great War: Stories Inspired by Objects from the First World War*. In *The Book of Pearl*, Timothée once again takes the reader on a journey to imaginary worlds in his typically elegant, beautiful and accessible writing style.